Jack Rubin is a police officer. He is dismissed after five years, accused of accepting bribes. He sets up in business as a private investigator and soon finds that his main occupation is to collect bad debts and harass vulnerable losers. However, his luck seems to turn when he takes on Mohammed Ali Malik, a Pakistani, as his partner.

Rubin, an atheist from a Jewish family, is a totally amoral tough guy and womaniser, and Malik, a Muslim and family man, loyal, frightened of his own shadow, are chalk and cheese. Yet, in spite of deep differences, their partnership seems to succeed. They have agreed one rule: never to discuss religion - and always to make their own tea and coffee.

CHEKHOV'S GUN

Jack Rubin

CHEKHOV'S GUN

EMMA
STERN
PUBLISHING

An Emma Stern Publication

ISBN: 978-1-911224-04-4

This is a work of fiction. Names, characters, places and incidents originate from
the writer's imagination. Any resemblance to actual persons, living or dead, is
purely coincidental.

Published in 2016

Emma Stern Publishing
107 Fleet Street
London
EC4A 2AB

www.emmastern.com
www.facebook.com/emmasternpublishing
Email: editorial@emmastern.com
Email: marketing@emmastern.com

Printed in Great Britain

Chapter One

I was only a messenger.

Delivering a message for Ives.

I had to meet this guy in Canning Town. I discovered that he was attending a party.

I parked my motor car in Woodford Green and took the Underground train to the East End. I found a taxi and the driver knew the street.

'This is a black area,' the driver said.

It was too. It was early evening when I arrived, warm, and many people were sitting outside. There was a regiment of children, shouting and laughing, kicking footballs and each other in the open street.

When I got out of the taxi there was a general hush. I paid the driver. I felt like a bottle of milk in a sea of Guinness.

I joined the party. Not a white face to be seen. A middle-aged woman greeted me.

'Can I come in?' I asked.

'If you're a friend,' she said, wiping her hands on her apron.

'What do I have to do to be a friend?' I asked, smiling openly.

She looked at me with suspicion in her eyes.

'Sawubona,' I said.

'Yebo sawubona.

'Unjani?' I said, asking her how she was.

'I am well. How can we help you?'

'Offer me a beer and a leg of chicken,' I said, and flashed my teeth.

'Come in, my friend,' she told me.

The kitchen was occupied by young women preparing food, putting it on plastic plates. The front room was full of older women gossiping and laughing, pausing only to clock the white guy greeting them in Zulu. They applauded me.

I passed on to the back garden, a grassed area. Here there were only men. There was initial silence.

'Christ,' I said, loudly, 'I feel like a bottle of milk in a sea of Castle lager.'

That isn't recycling a chestnut; nothing wrong in suiting the words to the audience.

That's all it needed and I was made welcome, and they were decent enough to converse with me in English, which was as well for I had exhausted my Zulu greetings.

'A young girl came into the garden and curtsied in front of me.

'Can I help you, Sir?' she asked, shyly.

There was silence still; I held the stage.

'How old are you?'

'Fourteen, Sir.'

'Come back in two years and I'll have something for you,' I said.

Vulgar, yes, but enough to please the men, already well oiled with bottles of Castle.

'A plate of food, my dear,' I continued. 'Pap, chicken.'

A couple of hours passed. After the first Castle I switched to soft drinks. I made conversation outside with men and finally moved inside the crowded house to chat to the women.

Eventually I found myself in a corner with an attractive black woman. After the prelims and pleasantries I asked her if she knew Danny Muggs. Her face changed: no smiles now.

'I take it that's a Yes,' I said.

The girl looked round nervously.

'Forget Danny,' she warned. 'He's not one of us. He's Carib.'

'I know all about him,' I said. 'I want to do business with him.'

The girl looked at me quizzically.

'You a user?'

I shook my head. 'Never touch that shit,' I said. 'It turns your brains to pap.'

'So why are you asking about Danny?'

There was a look of suspicion in her eyes.

I shook my head and smiled. 'I'm not a cop. I'm just a messenger.'

And that was the truth. Ives was paying me to deliver a message. No problemo, except the content of the message, which, put succinctly, read: Pay up, fucker, or you're dead black meat.

Ives may have been black himself but he was, like Danny Muggs, of the Carib line, not the African. Not that it mattered: no matter your origin, if you owed money to Ives, if you tried to muscle in on his territory, girls or narcotics, you had some serious explaining to do. Probably the best outcome would be a couple of broken legs. If you were a mutant with three legs, expect a triple fracture.

The girl said she had to return to the kitchen and help dish out the food. I didn't believe her but so what…..

I had only to wait about thirty minutes. I went into the sitting room and acted friendly with the older women, mothers and biddies. Like all charmers – and I know how to put on the charm as well as the frighteners - I can be a lying bastard.

From there to the bog. The soft drinks had filled my bladder. I opened the door, turned to shut it.

'Wey yu a go, white bwaay?'

I looked up, too late, found myself under attack from two black guys. I fought back but I never stood a chance. The confined space, the weight of the big guy, who hit me hard, often and low. My cods were being turned to mince.

'He's all yours, Danny,' the big guy said when I was on the floor and close to losing consciousness. I was being transported on the back of a blue winged elephant carrying me to a purple room where alligators were playing tenor saxophones.

Danny Muggs had a blade at my throat.

'Chobble nu nice, bwaay,' he said. And then, so's I could understand, he added, 'So, you wanna talk to me.'

It wasn't a question. He had learned I'd been asking. Some bird in the house had sung to him.

'I need water,' I croaked.

Danny Muggs laughed. 'Fuck you,' he said.

'I'm only a messenger,' I said.

'Who sendin' me messages, bwaay?'

'Ives.'

Danny turned to his pal, guarding the top of the stairs. Anybody wanted a piss, they'd have to go outside into the back garden.

Tell me, white bwaay. What dis message from Mr Ives?'

He had moved the blade away from my throat, so I was able to speak more clearly.

'Ives said to tell you, Danny, he wants the money you owe him.'

'Or?'

'What?'

'Or else?'

'He didn't say anything about an or else, Danny.'

'OK, OK. Ives innah big chobble. You tell him dat. I got Leicester. I want Nottingham.'

'I'll tell him, Danny.'

I calculated that the more I called him by his name, the less chance of having my throat cut.

'Unnerstan', bwaay?'

'You want Nottingham. I'll tell Ives that, Danny.'

'Yeah. You tell that Grenada bastard me belly a yawn. Yu a fig gi Ives dat.'

Had I known Ives was from a Grenada family? And in this situation, with Danny Muggs keen to cut the white boy, did it really matter?

Danny hadn't frisked me and I considered shooting the bastard there and then. I was thinking fast. I shoot Danny

Muggs, I had to take down his giant pal. Then scarper down the stairs and outside. The chances of a prowling taxi being around were nil. No guns, Rubin, not this time. Play along.

'Stand up,' Danny said.

He could speak standard English when he wanted to.

I struggled to my feet.

'Another message for Ives,' he said.

Before I had chance to move or respond the blade was in his hand and arcing toward my face. I held up my right hand, by instinct, and it was a good one. His blade cut the back of my hand but the reaction saved my face.

Without another word Danny ran down the stairs, followed by his pal – no doubt his muscle - and out the front door. No way could I follow after.

I filled the washbasin with cold water, to clear the blood and ease the pain. Downstairs a woman - she said she was a nurse - bandaged my hand. There was no talk about contacting the law. Someone called a taxi. I was given a tot of whisky, put in a taxi, and was taken to where my motor was parked.

'What happened with the hand?' the taxi driver asked.

Chapter Two

The pain in my hand was giving me gyp.

My own fault. I should've known the bastard would use the blade. They all do. Lucky it was my hand and not my face or throat.

It was mid-morning but already hot. The tar was beginning to bubble. That wouldn't do the car tyres any good. I could see heat shimmering on the road, just like in Africa. You want to know about heat mirages, drive from Cape Town to Dar. You want to know about corrupt border officials, drive from Cape Town to Dar.

But this wasn't Africa, the land of my childhood and early youth. This was England in June. Last year the floods, roads turned into rivers, fields to lakes. They said it was global warming. Followed by month after month of hot sun from cloudless skies. They say that's global warming, too. Well, I say: global warming, my arse. Or your arse, if you prefer.

The tank was full, Elgar on the CD, the bag of toffee in the glove compartment. I was all set for a long drive. I'd not bothered to get on the motorway. Not even the old A1, the Great

North Road, where not all that long ago stage coaches rolled and footpads waited. I was taking the scenic route.

Then I saw this bird hitching a lift. I never stop for hitch hikers. Not unless they're women, not unless they're young, not unless they are lookers, not unless I think they'll shag.

No point in describing her too closely. If you're a guy, you'll only work up a lather. If you're a girl, woman, female – whatever they are called these day – you'll only be envious as hell. Enough to say she was young, slim and had a sulky look, which I like in a girl.

'Where you going?' I asked, winding the window down.

She reached over to open the car door. I could see her bra-less boobs. The door was locked; I'm not a complete idiot, not even where young birds are concerned.

'Dunno,' she said.

'You must have a destination.'

'North,' she said.

That could mean anything, considering I hadn't yet passed Potter's Bar.

'Northampton, Sheffield, Leeds, Newcastle, Edinburgh, Reykjavik…..the North Fucking Pole?'

She smiled. Had a good set of teeth.

'The North Fucking Pole,' she said.

I unlocked the door. She lost no time getting in, snapped on the seat belt, offered me chewing gum, which I declined, and made herself comfortable.

'You travel light,' I said.

'Yer what?'

'Where's your baggage?'

All she had was a brown handbag – looked as if it might be leather.

I saw a sign. Cambridge this way, Northampton that. Choices, always choices.

'You ever been to Cambridge?' I asked.

'Yer what?'

'Never mind,' I said.

She stuck another wafer of gum into her face, silently offered the packet to me, and when I refused again put it back in her handbag.

'What'd you do to your hand?'

'I cut myself shaving,' I said.

'No you didn't.'

'No, I didn't,' I said. 'I was at a party in…….some dump in the Isle of Dogs. A black guy carved me.'

'Did you diss him?'

'No, I didn't. And even if I had, that's no excuse.......here, wait a minute!'

I pulled over to the side of the road, mounted a grass verge.

'Get out,' I said. 'And don't say yer what?'

'Yer what?' she said.

'Get the fuck out this car,' I ordered her.

She got out. Looked even sulkier. I locked the car on central.

Now that I had a chance to look carefully I could see she had a good slim body, long legs that were tight under jeans, a leather jacket top, comfortable shoes. Her arse was firm and not too large or too small. Her face was clear – no make-up covering zits, no freckles, no high colouring. She was pale in a Pre-Raphaelite way. Not the kind of girl who spent too much time outdoors.

From her bag she took a cell phone.

'How old are you?' I asked.

I expected another Yer What but what she said was, 'Why? Does it matter?'

'It does to me,' I said.

'Why?'

'Well, because......'

'Because you plan to get inside my knickers, that it?'

'Something of the sort,' I said.

She smiled. 'Nineteen OK by you?'

'The truth would be even better.'

'Seventeen. Straight up. The whole truth and nothing but the……do I get the lift now? Or can't you wait to get in among them trees?'

'I can't wait to get in among those trees,' I said, 'but not because you're irresistible.'

'Then why?'

'Because…..I need a piss, and quick.'

'Want me to hold him for you?'

I ignored that, went behind a tree and a clump of bushes, and realised I could have done with some help. Taking out Percy with my right hand bandaged, was far from easy.

Back at the car the girl was messing with her cellular phone.

'Oh shit!' she said.

'Trouble?'

'Carl. He's just texted me.'

'Told you to get back or get lost?'

'Something like that,' she said.

'Look…..do you have a name?'

'Grace.'

'Your real name,' I said.

'Grace,' she repeated. 'What about you?'

'Rubin.'

'Is that your first name or your second name?'

'Yer what?' I said.

I reached over, took the cell phone away from her, switched if off, gave it back, locked the car, and looked straight ahead to the road. I was mostly driving with my left hand, because of the bandage on the right. If I'd had two hands I'd have placed my left paw on her leg, see how she reacted. I had no doubt I was going to shag her. I was also certain that her name probably wasn't Grace and if she was under seventeen, well, I'd asked her, hadn't I?

'So what really happened?'

'With?'

'Your hand.'

'I told you. A black guy carved me.'

'There must have been a reason.'

'There's always a reason,' I said. 'Some people like killing, maiming, beating. Just for the hell of it. And I was a white man at a party where the other thirty-nine were all black.'

'So what's the reason you picked me up? What make is it, anyway?'

'Toyota,' I said.

'Old guy's motor.'

'In my case, poor man's motor,' I said.

'Whatever!' She smiled, not a big grin, not all mouth and teeth. 'You picked me up because you want…...to have sex with me.'

I didn't expect her to phrase it like that.

True or false, Rubin?'

'True,' I said, and risked steering with the bandaged hand again, so's I could place my left paw on her bejeaned thigh.

I saw a road sign. Another decision to make. Cambridge or Ely.

'Cambridge or Ely?' I asked her. 'We can find a bite to eat.'

'I've never been to Ely,' she said.

I signalled just in time, made my turn to the right, and we were along a flat road to Ely.

'I've never been to Cambridge either,' she said. 'But nosh is nosh, innit?'

'Use the word nosh a lot, do you?'

'Not always.'

'Did you know it's a Yiddish word?'

'What's that?'

'Never mind,' I said.

The tar on the road still bubbled. Suddenly the motor veered to the left.

'Shit!'

'A blow out?' she asked.

Chapter Three

We were close to a garage, an old kind of rural place. No phalanx of customer-operated pumps, no offers to wash and wax the vehicle, no shop selling sandwiches, drinks and chocolate at inflated prices. I pulled in. Better to change the wheel, if it were a puncture, off the road, and better to use a large jack than the small one in the boot compartment. Truth to tell, with the continuing pain in my right hand I needed a helping hand.

I got out. There was an old sign saying HEREWARD MOTOR REPAIRS. Nobody made an appearance. Whoever Hereward was, he didn't seem to be awake today.

I looked at the front nearside wheel. Sure enough, the tyre was going down.

After a few moments I reached into the car and sounded the horn. It needed two blasts. Maybe the guy was under a vehicle or on the can. Either way he ought not to ignore potential customers, especially as business did not appear to be going well.

From out of the station walked a skinny guy in overalls caked with grease and dirt.

That was all I needed: a yokel, an idiot grease monkey. I'd be lucky if he even had a jack.

'In some hurry, are you, mister?' he asked, taking in my appearance from beneath eyes with hooded lids, and, I noticed, also taking a good clocking of Grace, who'd climbed out for some fresh air.

'I have a puncture,' I said.

'Happens when it's hot like this,' the yokel said.

'As you can see, my right hand....'

You shouldna be drivin' like that,' the guy said.

'No, maybe not.' I paused. 'Can you help me?'

'You're not from these parts, are you?'

'No, we're travelling north,' I said. 'But we thought....well, I've heard Ely's a ......an interesting old place-'

'It is.'

'And my.....my sister and me, we need to eat.'

'Try the waterfront,' the man said. 'Good restaurants there. Bit pricey, though.'

'Thanks, we will,' I replied, wishing he'd get on with changing the wheel before I dropped dead with the heat or hunger or a combination of the two.

The yokel inspected the car minutely when all he needed was to jack up the front end, loosen the wheel nuts, change the tyre for the spare, tighten the nuts again, and let the jack down. Then I'd pay him and we'd be off.

'Fiver do you?'

I told him it would do me fine.

He wheeled out a jack and quickly changed the wheel.

'Now you don't have a spare,' he said.

He was one of those weary bastards who always sees the dark side of things. The sun is shining and the temperature's high and he'll be sure to tell you the weather's forecast to break next Tuesday.

'You sell these tyres?' I asked. I didn't expect he would, and expected to have to buy another tyre from a franchise in Ely.

'This was your problem, mister.'

He showed me a rusty nail. I took it from him and thanked him.

'You going to get a tyre in Ely?'

'Well, you didn't say you had one, did you?'

'I didn't say I had and I didn't say I haven't.'

Yokels! Same the whole world over. Smart arses.

'You don't need a new tyre. Waste of money.' He paused. Was he concluding, from the state of my ancient motor, that money or lack of it was crucial? If so, he was right. Business has not been too hot lately. Business is never too hot. 'I can vulcanise that hole,' he said.

'How much?'

'Another fiver. Two times five equals ten.'

'With or without?' I asked.

'That all depends,' he said, craftily.

'I don't work for Customs and Excise. I don't like to pay VAT. Straight ten, cash, no receipt needed. Right?'

'Right!' he said.

He took the tyre inside. The building was made of corrugated iron, zinc sheets, and must have been as hot as hell. I stayed outside with the bird, in what little shade the building afforded.

When he had finished the yokel came outside and put the spare in the boot.

'Want me to check under the hood?'

'The what?'

'Bonnet,' he said. 'Check radiator hoses, maybe. They split in hot weather.'

'Do you take debit cards?'

He shook his head slowly. 'Don't rightly like to use them. Don't rightly like to use banks either.'

'Well, I'm down to my last tenner, so the hoses will have to wait.'

I paid him the cash, he called me Sir, ogled the bird, and soon we were back on the road, heading for the fair city of Ely. Which isn't a bad sort of place, if you like that sort of thing. Which, it might surprise you, I do. Sure, I'm a man who has to live in a big city, among the high-rise buildings and the mean streets, and could no more live in the countryside than I could shag a sheep, which if I lived in the countryside might well be an option I needed to consider. Ely's a city, but not as we'd know it. The place is in fact very attractive, retains many historic buildings and winding shopping thoroughfares.

I parked the motor, paid the machine two quid. Long enough to have time to eat.

We walked slowly through the city centre, passed the cathedral – probably cool, in there, but I'd no intention of finding out – and down to the water. No need to follow signs. Keep going down and you'll find the river.

Grace was busy with her cell phone. I decided to let her witter. Carl or whoever she was texting, it didn't matter a fart. I was going to be the guy shagged her next.

I found a restaurant down by the river, paid for two, watched Grace eat like a horse, paid for two lagers, and an hour later wished I had been more.......what's the word? Circumspect. I was so full all I wanted was to go to bed.

'I'll find a place where we can book a day room,' I said.

'Day room?'

'Pay by the hour and then clear off,' I said.

'Sounds sleazy,' she said.

'You should know,' I said.

'So we find some little backstreet dump and-'

'No, we don't,' I interrupted. 'The best place for a day room is a large hotel. No luggage, book in, and two hours later leave again. No questions asked. OK with you?'

'Yeah!' she said.

'Now switch off that cell phone,' I said.

'And if I refuse?'

'I'll punch your fucking face, girl. Make a right mess of you.'

She switched off, looked at me for some seconds, and then said, 'You know, Rubin I think you really would.'

'You bet.'

'Like to thump girls, do you?'

'If you mean, do I get my rocks off from beating girls, no I don't.'

'How do you get your rocks off?' she asked, and she linked her arm in mine.

'That's for me to know and you to find out,' I said.

The hotel was large, out on the road to Cambridge. Part of a worldwide chain, and wild horses wouldn't drag the name out of me, but a handsome retainer might. I walked boldly to reception and said I wanted a day room for four hours.

'For two persons?' the foreigner at the desk asked.

They are always foreigners, like waiters in London restaurants. Who else wants a shitty job in the hospitality business?

I paid with cash. Yes, despite what I'd said to the yokel, I had a wad in my wallet.

Chapter Four

In the room there was air-conditioning. I took a shower and insisted that the bird join me. No way did I want her rifling my pockets while I was under the water. Her body was slim; not an ounce of fat. Yet she wasn't thin with it, and she had nice tits, which isn't always the case with slim birds.

I clocked her body all over. No complaints. Legs all the way from her ankles to her pert arse. No tattoos, which was a change. No scars.

I dried her off with a large white towel. She did the same for me. The towel was rough but her fingers were tender.

We lay naked on the bed.

'Rubin,' she said, 'can I ask you a question?'

'No,' I replied.

'You OK down there?'

'In what way?'

'Y'know. AIDS, HIV.'

'No problemo,' I said. 'You?'

'Clean,' she said. 'Carl checked me end of the month.'

'Carl checked you?'

'He's a doctor.'

I looked at her, that body, that pale face.

'I'm going to trust you. And you've got to trust me.'

'I trust you,' she said.

'Well, you shouldn't. But as it happens, I'm FFI. Free from Infection.' I paused. 'So we can go bareback.'

We started the foreplay.

'Rubin?'

'What now, for fuck's sake.'

'You really are a Jew, aren't you?'

'Look!' I said, starting to become angry.

'Well, you have been castrated.'

I laughed, pretended to make a quick check.

'Circumcised. That's the word. Castrated……it's more drastic.'

I tried to get back to the business in hand.

'Rubin?'

'For fuck's sake, Grace.'

'My name isn't Grace.'

'I never thought it was. Now shut your mouth and open your legs.'

'Don't you want to know what it is? Really, really is?'

'No!'

'It.....my name's-'

'I don't want to know!' I shouted.

I sat up. Looked at the Klimt reproduction on the far wall.

There were tears flowing from her eyes. The bird, not the Klimt repro.

'OK, what is it? Really, really!' I said wearily.

'Jen. Jennifer.'

'Right, Jennifer. Now understand this. I know women. I know you can turn the waterworks off and on, just like that. Tears don't impress me, kid.' I paused. The tears had stopped. 'Now let me ask you. How old are you? Really really!'

'Fifteen,' she said, looking at me suspiciously. 'But it's my birthday day after tomorrow.'

'Can you prove it?' I asked, disappointed as hell. I needed that shag.

She shook her head, told me she didn't carry a birth certificate.

'Well, Jen! We can either wait till Tuesday or I can let you have your present in advance.'

'You mean?'

'I mean I'm thirty-four and you're jail bait. So let's go.' I slapped her lovely bare arse. 'No more questions. OK?'

'Just one. Please. Tell me, why do you carry a gun?'

Chapter Five

I wiped the bandaged hand across my forehead.

The young bird seemed to be asleep. Young or not young, she hadn't been a virgin, though these days, what with bicycle saddles and strenuous exercise, it isn't always easy to tell. And as far as I'm concerned, it doesn't matter an Arab's fart.

I stared at the ceiling. Times like this I could kill for a ciggie. One of the true pleasures in this shitty life of ours, the post-coital smoke.

'What really, really happened to your hand?' Jen asked. She was awake after all.

'You don't want to know.'

Self-consciously I dropped my hand.

'Accident, was it?'

She snuggled up close to me.

'Don't be fucking nosy,' I said. And added: 'I need a drink.'

I looked for the mini bar. No good, not in this room, not at the bare price I'd paid. That meant water from the tap and that isn't always the right taste. You want water tastes good, you need soft water spilling down from the Pennines. Then, of course, the bastards in the water authority pollute it with chlorine and fluoride and, for all I know, Prozac. How else to account for the fact that a nation of free spirits and heretics has been transformed into sixty million docile pillocks whose only interests seem to be shopping and reading about slebs. Fuck the slebs, I say. I can't imagine, don't want to know, what it must be like to go to bed with a busty blonde and discover she isn't a blonde at all, and that gorgeous tit in your hand isn't flesh at all, but a lump of silicone, collagen, or whatever they implant in a woman's breasts.

As I walked back from drinking water I could feel Percy rousing himself again.

'Who's a happy boy, then?' the girl asked.

'That's what you do to me, babe,' I said, diving on the bed and getting on top of her, a tit in my good left hand.

She shagged like a rattlesnake. If she was not yet sixteen, then I'm Nebuchadnezzar, and I certainly am not. Knobbo, yes; Nebo, no. Jen knew all the tricks and then some more. By the time we'd finished second time round I was topside, finished, would have been as happy to die as the poor bastard chameleon is when he's so full of rapture he doesn't notice his mate is eating him, and spreading mustard on him for additional flavour.

I lay back on the bed. Wondered how many ceilings I've stared at in my life.

She got off the bed, went to the bathroom, left the door open, and started to do a jig.

'No need for that,' I told her.

'Yer what?'

'Standing up, making sure you don't get pregnant. It doesn't work anyway.'

'It's worked for me, so far,' she said, turning to look out at me.

'It doesn't matter,' I said. 'I had the snip.'

We took another shower together. This one was quicker. There's a world of difference between a pre-shag shower and a post. No lathering her secret places now, although this kid's secret had clearly been an open secret some time now.

As she dressed, she looked across at me, still naked.

'Rubin' she said, seriously. 'I really needed that. Ta.'

Men tend to think that they're the ones need sex in order to be stable and satisfied enough to carry on with life's work and tasks, but women need sex too. I don't mean all men and all women – can't speak for the whole world, can I? – but generally speaking, and in my experience.

'What next?' Jen asked.

'I'm motoring north,' I said. 'Leeds.'

'Come with you?'

'Sure,' I said.

'No Mrs Rubin in Leeds?'

'Stop asking questions and we'll both be happier,' I said.

'I won't be happier,' Jen replied. 'I like to ask questions. Like to know something about the guy who's just fucked me good and proper.'

'When a dog corners a bitch in an alley and gives her a quickie, does he ask about her background and pedigree? Eh? Does he?'

'We're not animals, Rubin,' she said earnestly.

'Oh yes, we are,' I said. 'The most dangerous animal on this planet.'

She shrugged. Checked her face in the mirror. Picked up her handbag.

'You have a gun, right? So why'd you let the other guy get near enough to cut you?'

I did not respond. I checked I'd left nothing behind.

The guy at Reception had nothing to say when I handed over the key, which wasn't a key but one of those cards you swipe into the lock. Not even a Thank you and Have a Good day, Sir. Of course he knew the reason why we'd been up in the room - it did not need a rocket scientist to explain that - but there was no call for dumb insolence. Unless he were a limp-wristed uphill gardener, and he did not appear to be, he probably envied me spending two hours in the arms and the vagina of this delectable little bird.

Chapter Six

The sun was sloping down in the sky but was still warm enough for discomfort. I opened all windows on the motor, letting in whatever cool air I could. The steering wheel was hot.

At last I was able to touch the wheel and steer out of the hotel car park. I came to a junction and took the road north toward Norwich. No reason, except that I really did want to take the scenic route.

Jennifer was quiet, eyes closed, maybe asleep. I was in no mood for conversation, and was not prepared to answer her questions. After a good shag, and it had been good for both of us, a period of silence is welcome. So that I wouldn't wake her, I did not play the CD, although the smoothness of Chanson de Nuit or Nimrod would have been pleasant. She'd have probably turned up that pert nose at my taste in music.

Funny how, in life, a sudden decision can make all the difference. Like now. I see a sign saying Afternoon Teas. I make a turn off the road on to a B road. The tar soon gives way to a dirt road.

Coming in the opposite direction, spouting dust into the afternoon air, a couple of racers. Ageing motor cyclists dressed like Goths, all leather except for bare arms.

The front guy was whooping, loud enough to be heard above the roar of his bike engine. Thought he was some kind of cowboy. Well, he was, but not the kind he wanted to be.

He was headed straight for my motor. I hauled over to the left, brushing hedges. Insects stirred, rose in panic. Jen woke up. Only at the last minute did the Goth pull away from a collision. His front wheel reared, it seemed he would fall off, but he kept in the saddle.

I mouthed the words, Fucking idiot!

No way could he hear me above the noise; my words were lost under the whine of the cycle engines.

I drew up outside a ramshackle dump. I'd made a mistake: this place had not served afternoon teas since the last years of the Edwardian period. Since moustached Elgar was composing his sublime music.

I turned the motor and made my way back. Why wasn't I surprised when in front of me, right in the middle of the track, grinning, sweaty, arms tattooed, the two fat Goths sat astride their Harleys, barring my way? I could have driven straight on and watched as the two of them scrambled to safety at the last minute, but I did not wish to damage my motor – bodywork costs, believe me.

Their engines were ticking over. It was possible to hear crows making their noise in a nearby tree. Noisy fucking birds and two nasty Goths. Welcome to the peace of the countryside. Like I said, I'm a city boy.

I stopped the car close to the bikers and switched off the engine. I said nothing.

By this time Jennifer was awake, close up to me; I could feel her tenseness.

'Yeah?' a Goth said.

I did not answer. Stared at him, straight in the eyes.

'You called me a fucking idiot.'

Still I did not respond. Silence can kill guys like these, no-brainers with Nazi tattoos.

'You hear me talking, mister?'

I sighed. How many B movies had this guy stared at in front of TV in the small hours?

Still I did not respond.

'Want the other hand bandaged?' he said.

One biker did all the talking. Maybe he was the butch one. I looked hard at the second Goth. What seem to be hard men are often hard women.

'You got a tongue, Jack?'

The talky Goth levered himself from the bike, slowly, as if from a horse. They also put a lot of Westerns out on TV in the graveyard hours. He'd seen too many.

He heaved the machine on to its stand. Fast and easily. Clear to me the guy had some strength, wasn't all blubber.

He strolled slowly and deliberately to the passenger side. Jen moved closer to me.

'Hi kid!' he said.

Jen did not answer. She was afraid. This surprised me: I'd had her card marked as a toughie.

'I said Hi. You got no tongue, slag?'

'OK,' I said. 'Enough already.'

'Enough already,' he mimicked, as if I were speaking in a pansy way.

'Get out of our way,' I said. 'We move off. No hard feelings.'

'No hard……who the fuck are you, Jack?'

He walked round to the front of the motor.

'I've warned you,' I said.

'What you say, Jack?'

He did not take his eyes off Jen. He stuck out his tongue in a leering lascivious way.

'My name isn't Jack,' I said.

Now at last he paid me attention.

'So what is it? Droopy drawers?'

His pal, who'd remained astride his vehicle, engine ticking over, ready to move away if things turned nasty, laughed a loud mirthless laugh.

'My name is Yehudi,' I said.

That stopped the Goth in his tracks.

'What kinda fuckin' name is that?'

'It's a Jewish name,' I said.

'You're a fuckin'.....?'

'Jew! Yeah! And you're a Nazi with shit for brains.'

It was then he drew the blade. Switch.

Grinning, he ambled his way round to my side.

'Right, Jew boy. We're gonna have to do some more cutting.'

'Del!' the other guy said.

His voice betrayed his concern but his pal ignored him.

Del, the Goth, was now close to me. I could see his sweat, almost smell his foetid breath, and could certainly see the switch blade close to me. Just when I thought he might reach out and cut me, or try to cut me, he stepped back.

'Hey! Tommy!'

He was looking at his pal now.

'Del?'

'What's the difference between a Jew and a canoe?

'I dunno, Del. What is the difference between a Jew and a canoe?'

They had played this routine before, I could tell.

'A canoe tips.' Del paused. 'Get it, Tommy: Get it?' He looked at me. 'Get it……Jew?'

I did not respond, not so much as the movement of an eye.

'OK, try this for size. What's the difference between a Jew and a pizza?'

'I don't know, Del,' I said. What is the difference between a Jew and a pizza?'

I'd heard this one before. I've heard 'em all.

'The pizza doesn't scream when you put it in an oven!'

He laughed obscenely.

I stepped out of the motor. He moved back, but still felt confident with the blade in his hand.

'Try this one, Del,' I said, and now I allowed a smile to appear on my lips, my heart cold, icy, despite the heat of the afternoon. 'What do you call a screwed-up biker, apart from mummy's boy, wanker, cock sucker and someone who takes it up his arse?' I held up my left hand, to silence him. 'And what do you call this cock sucking arse bandit when he has a hole in his gut?'

He sprang forward. He never made it. The sound of the shot seemed loud. He fell down on the dry earth, a look of surprise on his face. The pain in his gut would kick in later.

I turned to Tommy or whatever his name was.

'Peace, mate,' he said.

'Fuck off,' I said.

He opened the throttle and fucked off as fast as his wheels would take him.

Jennifer was out of the car.

She looked at me with a mixture of fear, pride and surprise.

The Goth was on his knees, crying out with pain.

'Now you know what it feels like to be a cock sucking arse bandit with a hole in his gut,' I said, and kicked him so that he fell backwards and away from the motor.

Chapter Seven

We were soon back on the main road. Now I felt pain in my right hand.

'You sneaky…..' Jen said.

'Sneaky?'

'The gun, it was in the bandage.'

'Not until he pulled the blade out,' I said.

'We going to call an ambulance?'

'Like fuck, we are.'

She was silent for at least ten seconds, which for her was a long time.

'You told me you're not a Jew,' she said.

'I'm an atheist,' I told her. 'Never go near a synagogue.'

She was silent for another ten seconds. Then she stroked my left arm.

'I've a confession to make,' she said.

'I don't want to know.'

'I'm not fifteen, going on sixteen.'

'Jesus, don't tell me. You're only twelve.'

She smiled. 'I'm twenty in two days time.'

'Then why'd you pretend to be fifteen?'

'Some guys like it that way. Gets them going.'

'Some guys prefer maturity,' I said.

'You still fucked me,' she said.

'I'd a lot of mucky water to get off my chest.'

She scowled, then smiled. 'I've never heard it called that before,' she said.

I drove up through the flat lands of East Anglia, skirted the Wash, turned west to Doncaster, then north to Garforth and on to Leeds.

I pulled into the centre of the city. It was evening now and parking was easy.

We went to the railway station. What for some daft reason people have taken to calling train stations. Wetherspoon's was packed, inside and out. They can't all have been commuters.

I ordered drinks, searched in vain for somewhere to sit, and finally parked my arse outside on the concrete, against the wall of the building. Jen did the same. She only took soft drinks, I noticed.

After an hour, I asked her if she were ready to eat.

'I'm always ready to eat,' Jen said.

'OK, let's hit the tarmac,' I said.

I drove up to Allerton and a Punjabi restaurant I've been to before, and liked. I ordered lamb and spinach. Jen ordered beef and rice. Two naan breads were one naan too many. I ate both, washed down with beer.

It was dark when we finally stepped outside, the last customers to leave.

'What are your plans now?' I asked, knowing well enough she probably had no plans.

She shrugged her thin shoulders.

'Want to stay the night with me?'

'You got a place here in Leeds?'

'No.'

'So?'

'We can find a hotel.'

I had no wish to go home to a cold cottage on the edge of the Pennine hills.

'Must cost a bomb.'

I parked, took a case and my laptop from the boot. I gave both to the girl, because of my bandaged hand, and because I'm a male chauvinist pig. I pay for her lunch, I pay for the evening meal, so this was the least she could do for me. I marched in to Reception.

'Small double,' I said.

The Receptionist, an attractive woman about my own age, with dark skin, shining hair – she might have been an Asian, or anywhere from the eastern Med – looked at me carefully, and then clocked Jen.

'We have a small double at the back, Sir,' she drawled.

'How much?'

'One hundred and twenty.'

'I'll give you forty,' I said.

'I'll have to ask the manager.'

'No, you won't. First, he's not on duty. He went home as soon as he possibly could. Second, that room will stay empty, so it's better to take forty quid from me than nothing at all. Agreed?'

'OK,' she said.

'That is bed and breakfast,' I said.

'No, room only.'

I was going to argue but decided against it. This room, does it have a safe?'

She checked her computer screen.

'336. Yes, a safe, a TV, and......two single beds.'

I paid with my debit card. Don't hold much truck with credit cards or cheque accounts. I'm strictly a cash man. I could have settled the room in cash but decided not to. I hate going to the ATM, or standing in line at the bank.

'Go on up, Jen,' I ordered. 'I'm just going to the bar.'

'You'll have to be fast,' the receptionist said. 'It's closing.'

I gave the door card to Jen. '336, can you remember that?'

She declined to answer.

I saw her into the Otis box, pressed for level three, and hopped out before the door slid closed.

At the bar there was a single customer, a guy who looked anything but happy. He had the face of a man who hasn't farted for a year.

'Double brandy and ginger ale,' I told the barman. 'No ice.'

'No ice?'

'There's an echo in here,' I said.

'No life here,' the melancholy guy said.

I'm never happy talking to strangers in bars, least of all when they are of the male gender.

'I'm not looking for life,' I said. 'I'm looking for a good night's sleep.'

'That your girl friend you came in with?'

'No, my sister. But we sleep together.'

He looked surprised.

'Keep it in the family, I always say.'

That was the end of that conversation.

My cell phone rang.

I picked up my drink, went and sat down well away from the bar.

'Yes?'

'Mr Rubin?'

'Yes. Who's this?'

'Ives.'

'Oh, hello…..Ives. How's tricks?'

'I gotta see you,' Ives said.

'Save it till tomorrow, Ives. I'm just getting into bed with a nice-looking little bird.'

'It's gotta be now,' Ives said.

'No can do, my friend. Tomorrow.'

'But I'm close by,' he said.

I could sense from his voice he was enjoying this.

'How close is close?' I said, believing he was trying to suss out exactly where I was.

'Looking in from the car park,' Ives said, and he laughed.

I peered out. There he was. All six-foot six inches of hard man. Last thing I needed was to be leaned on by a fucking gangster high as a skyscraper and built solid like a Centurion tank.

I finished my drink and walked to Reception. The dark-skinned woman was pretending to be busy. Ives came in through the door.

'All alone, Ives?'

'Two guys in the motor,' he said. 'Got a room?'

'Yes,' I sighed.

'Then let's go.'

'No visitors after ten o'clock, Sir,' the receptionist said.

Ives took out a wad. From the same shoulder he usually packs a gun. He peeled off fifty.

'That cover it?'

'The woman shrugged. 'Breakfast is extra.'

'I won't be staying for breakfast,' Ives said. 'Less than one hour. This is a business meeting. It won't take long.'

We walked up the steps. As usual Ives was dressed to the nines, smart long black coat, collar and tie, for all the world like a successful businessman. Well, he is in business, that's true enough. Except his business is putting pressure on guys who don't deliver, or tarts who think they can cream part of their earnings off the top.

'What happened to the hand?' Ives asked as we walked the corridor to 336.

'I was saying goodnight to my girlfriend and she closed her legs,' I said.

Ives smiled.

I knocked on the door. Jen came to open it.

She was naked. Had to be, because she travelled light.

'This the one did damage to your hand?' Ives laughed.

Jen walked back to bed. No rush, no attempt to hide her nakedness.

'Hello, darling,' Ives said.

Jen did not answer.

'What's the matter with her, Mr Rubin?' He laughed. 'Cat got her tongue?'

'Go to sleep, Jen,' I said. 'Now, Ives, I think I know your next question.'

'Yeah! What happened to your hand?'

'And the next question?'

'Yeah! What went wrong in Canning Town?

Chapter Eight

The gutters were clogged up with tin cans, cigarette packets, soft drink cartons and the detritus of takeaway chicken, chips and curried this and that. This was chav land. Mean streets, hostile residents. Don't give me any shit about community spirit. These people are mean, stupid and moan twenty-four hours a day, even in their sleep.

At the entrance to Laurel Street – if they're named for plants the places are Grotsville – there was a guy dressed in ragged clothes. Next to him was a flea-bitten mongrel that looked as if it could do with a good meal.

'Anybody there?' the man asked me.

'Are you talking to me?' I asked.

It was enough to come down to this shit factory without being accosted by a fucking beggar.

'Is there anybody else there?' he asked.

For a guy who was about to touch me for the price of a cup of tea, which he'd then spend on whisky or whatever his poison was, he was being surprisingly aggressive.

'I've no money, mate, if that's what you're after,' I said.

'I'm not your mate,' he said, looking straight ahead.

'Thank Christ for that.'

'Aint yer got no respec' for a blind man?' he said.

'Sure,' I said, 'in the right place, at the right time. And sitting on your arse in this fucking midden isn't the right place.'

'I want yer to get me a drink from the corner shop,' he said.

'Can't you walk down there yourself?'

I was stupid, allowing him to draw me into a conversation in this way. The wise thing would have been to walk away.

'Lemonade,' he said. 'Big bottle o' pop.'

'You got here without me. You must know where the corner shop is.'

'Where is it?' he said, the strong edge still in his voice.

'It's on the corner,' I said.

'It's not too much to ask, is it?' he whined.

I reached over and removed his dark glasses.

'Hey, what the fuck?'

His eyes seemed fine enough but that's no way of knowing, just looking. Blindness comes in many forms.

I fished in my pocket and took out two coins, a pound and a two quid coin. In my left hand I placed the pound and in my right the two pounds.

'Which one do you want?'

'That one,' he said, pointing to the two quid.

'You wazzack,' I said, 'you're no more blind than I am.'

I trousered the coins again.

'What happened to your hand?' he asked.

'You don't care what the fuck happened,' I said.

Nobody in this rotten world cares for anybody. If my mother had really cared, she wouldn't have done a bunk from South Africa, leaving my Dad all alone. If my Dad had cared for his wife and son he would not have boasted about the number of black girls he'd shagged. If I'd cared about Jennifer – and give me one good reason why I should – I'd not have let her leave the previous evening with Ives, who'd not treat her well and would within a week have her out on the streets, part of his stable of tarts earning good money for him. If Jen had cared a jot for me – and why should she, for Chrissakes? – she'd have refused to leave with Ives, leaving me to sleep alone. Not that I had, for no sooner had I seen Ives and his new doxy off from the front entrance of the hotel, than the receptionist had locked the door for the night, turned down the lights, and accepted my invitation to 336. It's a terrible world, when you come to think of it. We are born, we suffer, and then we die. We are here as on a darkling plain, swept with confused alarms of struggle and flight, ignorant as those armies that clash by night.

'I was in the army,' the guy called after me. 'The Gulf War.'

I did not stop to ask which one. He'd probably never seen a weapon, never donned a uniform. This kind of scrounging underclass scum can lie at the drop of a hat.

I knocked on the door of number 6 Laurel Street.

A face appeared at the window. I gestured for her to open the door, managed a smile too, to put her at ease. It worked.

Tracey Munden was clearly a slag. Pram face. Thin body, in need of exercise, toning; pale face, scraggy neck; hair that seemed not to have been washed or brushed in ten years; thin legs that might have looked better on a crane fly.

I showed her my card. Said it was about her debt and suggested she might like to let me in. We didn't want the neighbours and all that. She opened the door. It seemed as if she'd soaked the carpets with engine oil about two hours earlier. There was the pervading stink of stale food. In a house there is always going to be the smell of food, but this was rank, stale, foetid, rancid – choose your word, they all mean pretty much the same.

Where women were concerned, I have never been too fussy, but even I draw lines. Tracey was one such line. Nostalgie pour la boue, it's a longing for the gutter, a compulsion that comes over people when they have, for complex reasons, a need to immerse themselves in self-degradation. It's usually a mix of drink, drugs, and sex. It is said that Napoleon used to write to Josephine and instruct her that he'd be home in about four weeks and not to bath. There are times when I can understand the compulsion. But Christ, I have my limits. Nostalgie pour la boue is one thing; wallowing in shit and sperm with this pale slag would be another.

'Mrs. Munden -'

'Tracey. Call me Tracey.' She sniffed.

Call me…..Ishmael, I thought.

'Tracey, I'd like to talk about your outstanding debt.'

'That bastard Jason,' she said, though not with any strong emotion. 'Fancy a cuppa? Tea? Coffee?'

I said I'd have a glass of cold water. From the tap. It was another hot day. Truth was, whatever came out of the tap, any tap, was bound to be cleaner than anything from Tracey Munden's kitchen.

'Now Tracey, you've been a naughty girl, haven't you?'

'Have I?'

'You promised to keep up with your payments but you've missed. Repeatedly. Which is why I'm here.'

'You from the finance company?' she asked.

'Yes,' I said.

That wasn't true. I work as a private investigator. That may sound as if I'm some sort of private detective, which is sometimes true, but much of the time I chase debts, threaten people in different degrees, follow errant spouses. Oh yes, you'd be surprised how many people want their other half following, checking on. Without adultery I'd not be doing such good business. Am I doing good business? Well, it varies. Sometimes the wallet is full of notes. Other times, I'm doing work for gangsters like Ives. The winter months are never good but things look up in spring. Sometimes I do background checks, personal and corporate, surveillance, fraud, due diligence. I like to call it legal and litigation support services. It all beats working in a call centre or doing a McJob. I tell you!

'You've got kids, Tracey, right?'

She sat down and lit a ciggie. They may be poor, even desperate, but they can always afford a packet of cigs.

'Smoke?'

'No,' I said. 'Kids, Tracey. How many?'

'Three.'

'Who's going to look after them if you go down?'

'Down?' She look startled.

'If you don't cough-'

'Cough?'

'Pay some money. If not, you're going to prison.'

She took a deep drag on the cigarette, put on a stubborn look.

'I could do the time.' Again that annoying sniff.

'You think?'

'Sure.'

'Caged up with fucking butch lesbians who haven't been out for years? Sticking objects in your........ That what you want? Fisting you till you're raw. Not once but night after night. That what you want, Tracey?'

She shook her head.

'So I need cash. Now. Before I leave. Fifty quid.'

'I aint got fifty,' she wailed.

'Yes, you have. You drew over a hundred and sixty at the post office this morning. After you'd dropped Ashley off at school. Round to the post office to draw the child benefit.'

'You had me followed?'

'Not me Tracey, love. The people I work for.'

'Do they mean it?'

'This time, yes. They're bad bastards, Tracey. But I want to help you. Give me fifty, and I'll take the heat off.'

'You really had me followed from the school to the post office? I didn't notice.'

I didn't tell her it was me. I was the good cop, keeping her out of the clutches of the bad cops.

She stubbed out the dog end.

Then the stupid bitch fluttered her eyelashes at me, or tried.

'Is there any way we can.....you know......reach an agreement?'

'What you trying to suggest, Trace?'

'Y'know.'

'No, can't say I do know.'

'Make it twenty-five and we can have a quickie?'

Twenty-five quid for a quickie with Tracey when I'd enjoyed it for free, cost of meals apart, from Jen?

I shook my head.

'Blow job?'

'Do you swallow?'

'I can do.'

I shook my head sadly.

'No can do, Trace. More than my job's worth.'

'The fucking milkman does.'

'I'm a married man, my dear. Four kids of my own. I'm a one-woman guy, y'know.'

'Fifty quid, you say?'

'That, or it's the baseball bats.'

'What?'

'Well, maybe not literally. But they'll have the skin off your hide, believe me.'

She lifted up a cushion, opened her purse, took out fifty quid.

I grabbed it. Job done, time to get out into fresh air.

I stopped at the door. Where are the two other kids, Tracey?'

'With a neighbour.'

'You pay her to look after them?'

'I have to. I was losing me marbles, wasn't I?'

'Try to get off the drugs, Tracey,' I said.

'I'm not on dope,' she said, sniffing.

I walked back along Laurel Street. The old geezer was still sitting there, his dark glasses on, pretending to be blind. It was a daft place to beg; everybody in that area must have known he was a con man, not blind at all.

I stopped, reached down and petted the old man's dog. It felt cold.

'I think you'd better give your mutt some food, old man,' I said.

'Why?'

'He looks sick.'

'He's not sick.'

'His body's cold,' I said.

'There's a reason for that,' he said.

'What?'

'He's fuckin' dead, aint he?' and he laughed.

'What the hell....why are you keeping the body of a dead dog?'

'He only just died..... about two hours ago.'

'You sick twat,' I said.

'No need for that, mate. And tell me....'

'Yes?'

'The bandage, what happened to your hand?'

'I thought you said you're blind.'

'Visually impaired,' he said. 'Give us a quid, can't you? I'm hungry.'

'Eat the fucking dog,' I said.

I continued back to where I'd parked the motor. No way was I going to bring it in to Laurel Street. The bastards would have stripped it to the bone within minutes of me entering Tracey's house.

My cell phone rang.

'Mr Rubin?'

'Speaking.'

It was a female, young to judge from her voice.

'You don't know me but-'

'What do you want?' I interrupted.

'Tonight. Mr Gledhill wants to meet with you.'

I said nothing. Silence always fazes them.

'Mr Gledhill. You've heard of him, haven't you?'

'No, can't say I have.'

'But I thought everybody knew of Harry Gledhill.'

'Where does he want to meet me?'

'Telos Club and Bar. Know where it is?'

'Time?'

'Eight.'

'Will do,' I said.

'You sure you've never heard of Mr Gledhill?'

I switched off.

Harry Gledhill. Who hadn't heard of Happy Harry? In a city of bad bastards, Happy Harry was among the worst. When Happy Harry calls you in for an audience, if you have any sense in your head you turn up.

Chapter Nine

I told the taxi driver to stop at the Telos Club and Bar. Paid him and waited for my change. The driver, a fat Pakistani - all taxi drivers in this city are of Pakistani family origin - short-changed me by fifty pence. I held out my hand.

'Fifty pence.'

I never shorten it to the single letter 'p'.

'What's that?' the driver said.

'Fifty pence short.'

'I have to make a living,' the cab driver said.

'I'll decide if you get a tip, mister,' I said.

'And do I?' the fat guy asked.

He passed over the fifty pence.

'Like fuck, you do,' I said.

No driver was going to decide what the size of a tip would be. No way.

The taxi driver gave me a look that was pure hatred, switched off the car's interior light, and drove away to find his next fare.

I shrugged. About tipping, I never varied. Don't fucking give them.

I walked into the public bar. It hardly seemed to be buzzing. But who can tell? Later, I might get lucky.

'Beer or hard?' the barman asked, barely bothering to look at me. The man's hand was already hovering at the beer pump; he had marked me down as a beer drinker. The way I was dressed, the guy probably thought I couldn't raise the price of a short. I noted the look of contempt. Twice in five minutes, I thought. Fuck me, why do I bother?

'Rock shandy,' I said.

This time the barman did look at me.

'Don't think I know that one, mate,' he said.

That was what I had expected. There are many ways of reducing a stroppy bastard in size.

'It depends where in the world you are,' I said. 'In Ireland, it's fizzy orange and soda, half and half in a long glass. In South Africa, it's soda water and lemonade, fifty-fifty.'

'I'm busy,' the barman said. 'Which one you do you want, mate?'

'I want the Malawi variation,' I said. 'Long glass. Half soda water, half lemonade, with a few dashes of Angostura bitters.' I paused. 'Think you can manage that….. mate?'

I sat down on a bar stool.

'Ice with that?' the barman asked.

'No ice,' I said.

I looked round. The place wasn't full by any measure. Men and women sat together, men sat in pairs too, but there didn't appear to be any spare birds. There were a couple of booths, but I didn't expect any spare in those. Why was I thinking of getting my end away? Because sex is like drugs – addictive.

The barman brought the rock shandy. I tasted it and was satisfied. It wasn't real lemonade – it had come through a tube – but at least the soda water had come from a tin, and the bitters gave the drink a bite it would otherwise have lacked.

A man came over and sat on the stool next to me. He was about the same age as me– early thirties – but he had a developing beer gut, while I am in good physical shape. Need to be, the company I keep.

'You alone?' the guy asked.

'No, I'm with my friend here?'

The man looked round.

'He's a large invisible giraffe,' I said. 'Not everybody can see him.'

'You're pulling my pisser,' the man said, smiling foolishly.

'You should be so lucky,' I said, taking a drink.

'What's that?'

'What's what?'

'The drink you're……er…..'

'Drinking?' I asked, my voice as sour as the Angostura bitters. 'Is that the word you're searching for?'

'Yeah.'

'Rock shandy,' I said, 'and no, I don't want to give you the recipe.'

'Alcoholic, is it?'

I shook my head and emptied the glass in one final gulp. I managed to catch the eye of the peripatetic barman.

'Same again,' I said.

The barman took down a clean glass.

'Lemonade, soda water, and a dash of –'

'That's right,' I interrupted.

The man sitting at my side smacked his lips together audibly.

'You wouldn't like to……er…..?'

'No, I fucking would not,' I said. 'I never buy drinks for men.'

'Only women?' the guy said dolefully.

'You catch on quick,' I said.

I paid for the rock shandy. Exact money. I don't like walking around with coins in my trouser pockets. That way, you get holes in the pockets and then you can't put coins in them. There was probably a Law about that, some philosophical principle that I had not learned about at school. The Rubinenberg-Humdinger Principle, I thought, and smiled.

'Share it,' the guy said.

'What?'

'You smiled. I thought you'd like to share the joke.'

'You thought wrong,' I said.

'You're not very friendly, are you?' the guy said.

'Not with ponces who come over and try to bum me for the price of a drink,' I replied.

'You calling me a ponce?' the other asked.

He stood up. It was clear from his red face and his feigned anger that he was spoiling for a fight. I wasn't worried. Never fear the man with a red face. Fear the one whose face is as pale as putty, for with him the blood has drained from the periphery and gone to serve his muscles.

'I'm calling you a ponce and a cadger,' I said. 'And if it's a fight you want, you can have it in here or outside. Either way, you lose……ponce.'

The barman was paying attention now. Two or three customers could hear what I was saying, and they were listening too, looking forward to a scrap. It was a bit early in the evening, the barman thought: fights usually erupted about ten or eleven, when a lot of alcohol had been consumed, and two guys wanted to impress a bird.

The man said nothing. I could see him relax and his belly sag a little. The belly, that was where I would have struck first. Not the face, as others did, but a solid strike to the solar plexus, just below the midriff where blood vessels and nerves radiate. One good punch there and most guys go down. And it would have to be my left hand too.

The man wandered off to another part of the room, well away from the bar where I was sitting.

'He's a nuisance,' the barman said.

'You know him?'

'He comes in here often.'

'If he's a nuisance, ban him,' I said.

The barman snorted. 'He'd take us to court. Scream about his human rights.'

'Does he spend money?' I asked.

Bars are like casinos - don't like to ban good spenders.

'When he's been paid, yes. He's always talking to somebody,' the barman said.

He walked to the other side of the long bar, to serve a customer who was getting irate, having had to wait at least ten seconds to be served. What was it, I wondered, that made people get all testy when they had to wait more than a few minutes? Supermarket checkouts, bank service, waiting for a bus, people become fidgety and then aggressive. What was the hurry? Save a few minutes in order to get home and watch some crap soap opera on telly where people seem to be miserable all the time. Miseries watching misery. Welcome to chavland.

I am a patient man. I can sit down all day and watch paint dry, so long as I'm being paid. A lot of work I received was just that – watching, doing nothing. A wife who didn't trust her husband or partner, or a husband who suspected that as soon as he left for work in the morning every guy in the street was queuing up to shag his wife. I have seen the wives and know I'd have to be desperate even to look at most of them. As a private investigator, detective, inquiry agent – I have never found the title that best suits my activities - the time spent watching and waiting allows me to read a lot. I'm a member of a dying species: people who read books for pleasure. I love books. Not all books, of course, but anything, fiction or not, that takes my fancy, and my fancy these days is history and science. What I can't stomach are dreary novels by middle-class women who want to tell you why, surrounded as they are by wealth, they cannot find a meaning in life until they have an affair with a poncy Italian gondolier or a Cypriot fisherman who's AC/DC, and does not give a damn who knows it, and end up shagged and still not knowing the meaning of life.

For my part, I am convinced that there's no meaning to life, or if there is, we'll never know what it is. And not in Tuscany or

Paphos, for fuck's sake. Maybe I read too many science books. Or too much Nietzsche. In translation, of course.

My cell phone rang. It was Malik.

'What do you want?' I said.

'Where are you?' Malik asked.

'It's Friday evening. I'm busy lighting the Shabbat candles,' I said.

'I thought only the women lit the candles,' Malik said seriously.

'How the fuck would I know?' I said.

But I knew, for my mother had always kept the observance.

'So where are you?' Malik persisted.

'In the bar at the Telos,' I said.

'Why didn't you tell me? I could join you.'

'Will your wife let you out?'

'I don't need to ask her permission to do anything,' Malik replied, haughtily. 'I'll be down in about ten minutes.'

Malik did not take alcohol but had no problem with going into public houses or bars, so long as he could order soft drinks. Which was a nuisance for me, for soft drinks work out dearer than alcohol.

'Don't bother,' I said.

'What?'

In that single word there was disappointment.

'I'm hoping to get laid,' I said.

'You're always hoping -'

'How many times I get it or I don't get it, is no fucking business of......'

Chapter Ten

Suddenly, I was aware that a woman was standing close to me, listening to every word. It could have been the hint of perfume, or the way that even a person unseen inevitably changes the molecular structure of the air.

'Must go,' I said. 'Catch you later.'

'I'll ring you,' Malik said.

'Don't bother,' I told him. 'Just don't bother.'

On the woman's lips there was an amused smile.

'What are you drinking?' I asked her.

She could not have been much above twenty-four, twenty-five, the early twenties anyway, but she appeared to have poise. She was dressed in black skirt, black roll-neck jersey – tits firm beneath the wool – black stockings and black high-heel boots.

'How did you know black's my colour?' I said.

'I just knew,' she said.

'Sure you won't have that drink?'

'I have one already. Over there.'

'And who bought it for you?'

'He's sitting right over there,' she said.

There was a screen constructed of slatted wood, making a kind of small booth.

'And who is…..he? Your father, maybe?'

'He can hear every word,' she said, smiling.

'How's that? Got an ear-trumpet, has he?'

The girl grimaced and put a finger to her lips.

'You have a voice that's……'

She could not think of the word. Perhaps she was less intelligent than she looked. Not that the size of her brain mattered to me. I would have liked to shag her, not give her an IQ test.

'Stentorian?' I suggested.

'What?'

'Never mind,' I said.

'He wants to talk to you,' the girl said.

'I already have a date,' I said.

Again, the pained look on her face. Whoever the guy she was with, she had no wish to offend him.

She patted the palm of her left hand with the fingers of her right. I interpreted this as meaning whoever the man was, he had money. I mimed riffling bank notes. The girl nodded, barely perceptively, but clear enough for me to recognise.

'He'd like you to join us,' she said.

'Do you have a name?' I asked.

I expected her to say Tracy, or Jade, or Kylie, or some other name common among chavs.

'Wanda,' she said. Then, 'Are you coming, or what?'

'No, just breathing heavy,' I said.

I followed her to the booth. Sitting there, alone, looking displeased, was a middle-aged man wearing dark glasses and smoking a cigar, right under a No Smoking sign. Happy Harry Fucking Beat 'em up and Toss 'em in the river Gledhill. He motioned for me to sit down. I remained standing.

'Cllr. Gledhill? You asked to meet me. I'm Rubin.'

'Gledhill. Harry Gledhill. You may know the name.' He looked at me. 'I asked you to sit down.'

'There's a problem, Mr Gledhill.'

'What? You got piles or something?'

'Are you blind, Mr Gledhill?'

I saw Wanda wince. She swallowed hard. Clearly, nobody she knew talked to Happy Harry Gledhill in this way.

'You see, I have a problem talking to people in dark glasses. I have to see the eyes. You understand, don't you?'

'I'm keeping them on,' Gledhill replied.

I shrugged.

'Been nice meeting you,' I said. 'And you, my dear.'

I nodded toward Wanda and walked away.

'Wait!'

Gledhill was a man accustomed to giving orders. I was playing a dangerous game, I knew, but was playing it deliberately.

'Sit down,' Gledhill said.

And removed his dark glasses.

'Cigar?'

'Don't smoke, thanks,' I said, and sat down.

'Never?'

'I gave it up ten years ago,' I said.

'Why was that?' Gledhill asked.

There was whiteness about his eyes, suggesting he rarely removed the dark glasses. I notched that up as a victory. This guy wasn't going to call the shots.

'I found it was affecting my breathing,' I said. 'And it made my clothing stink. Also, my mouth felt like the bottom of a slop bucket that hasn't been emptied for about a hundred years.'

'You have a way with words, Rubin.'

I nodded but did not respond in words.

'I heard you,' Gledhill continued. 'The way you handled the drunk.'

'He wasn't drunk,' I said.

'Whatever. You handled him.' He paused, puffed on his cigar. 'Tell me, Rubin-'

'Mr Rubin if you don't mind.'

'You're an argumentative sod, aren't you?' Gledhill said, suppressing a smile.

'No,' I said.

'I could use you,' Gledhill said.

I did not reply. Let the guy get round to it, in his own good time. I was in no hurry myself. The night was still young and I was confident I'd get laid by midnight. After which, it didn't matter if the stately coach turned into a fucking pumpkin.

'Wanda,' Gledhill said.

I had noticed that the girl had her eyes fixed on me. She was sitting in a position where she hoped Gledhill wouldn't notice.

'Wanda, get the drinks in. What are you drinking, Mr Rubin?'

'Rock shandy.'

'Ah yes! I heard you instructing the barman, didn't I?' He gave Wanda a tenner from a thick wad. 'Same again for me and for Mr Rubin.'

As the girl walked away - walked not teetered, for the heels of her black boots were not so high she lost balance - I was careful to keep my eyes on Gledhill. Didn't want him to know what I was thinking, which was that of all the women in the world, I would at this moment like to be shagging the delectable Wanda.

'You don't smoke, and you don't drink alcohol. You're quite the good boy, aren't you?'

'I'm not a boy,' I said strongly. 'And what I do is my own business.'

'No need to be touchy, son,' Gledhill said.

'So long as we know,' I said. 'Just so long as we know.'

Gledhill looked round. Because of the booth, he could not see the whole room. Satisfied that nobody could hear, he leaned over conspiratorially and said in a soft voice, almost a whisper, but one made hoarse with cigar smoke,

'How would you like to work for me?'

Since passing the tenner to Wanda, Gledhill had been holding his wad. Now he shoved it back in his breast pocket.

I don't like people who flaunt their wad. Ives does it. Malik, too, when he has dosh. Malik's not alone – most Pakistanis do it. The message is clear: see how well I'm doing, and, look, it's in cash.

'I already have a job, Mr Gledhill. My own business. But if you have something that's up my street.....'

'I'm in business as well,' Gledhill said. 'You may have heard of me.'

He had said that already.

'Tell me,' I said.

'I make my living in a lot of ways. I'm in the process of branching out. But too many others are trying to muscle in on my operations.'

'Operations?'

'I've bought a piece of land. Out near the ring road. I'm going to open a restaurant at the top, with a car park on the first five levels. And a hotel. Plus some apartments. This city's on the up and up.' He paused, letting it sink in. 'Could be an earner, I think.'

'High rates, though,' I said. 'And security costs for the car park.'

'I'll do more than break even,' Gledhill replied smugly.

'I take it you don't see me as the manager of the new hotel or the restaurant,' I said.

Wanda returned with the drinks. As she passed my rock shandy across the table she looked straight and deep into my eyes. Message received and understood.

'Go and powder your nose, Wanda,' Harry Gledhill ordered.

'Eh?'

'The ladies room. Get lost. Don't hurry back.'

Wanda pouted but she obeyed.

'What do you think?' Gledhill asked.

'About the restaurant or the hotel?'

'Don't try and flannel me,' Gledhill said, a note of contained fury in his voice. 'About Wanda.'

'Nice looker,' I replied, trying to hide any enthusiasm I felt – and I felt plenty – 'you're a fortunate man, Mr Gledhill.'

'She's my big problem,' Gledhill continued. 'I can't be with her all the time. Business commitments, you know. Stamping on the opposition. And in any case, my wife wouldn't like it.'

He smiled, as if he were a sly comedian.

I smiled too. I never intentionally turn away the prospect of money.

'So how do you think I might be able to assist you, Mr Gledhill? You did mention working for you, right?'

Gledhill nodded. He puffed on his cigar.

'I like your style, Mr Rubin. Nobody pushes you about. You don't seem to be afraid of anyone.'

'That pot-bellied ponce at the bar?'

'No, me,' Gledhill said. 'Nobody else dares to tell me to take off my shades. You did. And I think you'd have walked away if I hadn't.'

Gledhill would get round to the point, eventually.

'I can buy protection whenever I want. Big black guys. Ex-soldiers. You know the kind of chap.'

I knew. Night club bouncers with shaven heads. Muscle for gamblers and big-time drug barons. Enforcers.

'I have my security. But I don't want that kind for this job. Understand?'

'No, I don't understand. I don't know what the job is, do I?'

'You strike me as the man I need. Tough but intelligent. Sober. Doesn't take shit. Won't give me any – you know, trouble.'

'And all that you concluded from eavesdropping with me and the ponce?'

'No, I made enquiries. Your name cropped up a couple of times.'

'I don't work cheap,' I said. 'And I don't do anything illegal.'

'No problem,' Gledhill replied.

'And I'm in business. So it would have to be contract work. Nothing permanent.'

'I'll pay you cash,' Gledhill assured me. 'Off the books. No problems with VAT and the tax man.'

I nodded. 'I can live with that, Mr Gledhill. So…..what's the job?'

At that moment, Wanda returned. It was clear that she had touched up her face, particularly her eyes. I didn't take that as a sign of interest, though: the girl had been told to bugger off to the ladies' room, and what else was there to do in there except titivate her hair and check her make-up? After she'd done what such rooms are principally for, that is.

I looked at her. She was attractive, and even without cosmetics and other assistance would still look pretty good. In ten years time she'd be running to fat but right now she was very presentable. I knew what I'd want from her. I entertain no nonsense about love and cherishing. Human beings are animals, and the name of the game is survival. Take what you can get; enjoy sensations; and you're a long time dead. I don't want any woman to fall in love with me, whatever that means; I want to shag them, satisfy them, and give myself freedom from physical pressures. Life is short and ends in death, but that doesn't mean we have to pass through our allotted span with long moping faces.

Wanda sat down. Crossed her legs. I could make out a glimpse of white thigh, accentuated by the black of her stockings. There was a suspender belt up there somewhere, I surmised. I like suspender belts but had noticed that elasticated stocking tops were generally favoured these days.

Gledhill patted Wanda's hand, a visible sign of ownership.

'I'm willing to pay you, and pay you well, to take care of Wanda for me.'

We discussed terms. It didn't take long. No written contracts, no trying to argue for better terms. He made an offer and I accepted. I told him I had other work to do and he said there'd be no problem so long as Wanda was protected.

We were going to shake hands on the deal. Then Gledhill said: 'What happened to your hand?'

Chapter Eleven

'Pay me to look after Wanda!' I said, laughing. 'Fucking hell! I'd pay him to look after her.'

Malik looked worried. Nothing new there, of course. He has the jowls of an out-of-condition bloodhound, and the ears to match. His face is that of a man who is an intimate friend of constipation.

'Gledhill's a gangster,' Malik said. 'And Wanda's his girl friend.'

'Wanda's a tart who goes where the money is,' I said. 'Or where she can get a good shag.'

'Don't fall foul of Gledhill,' Malik warned. 'He's a dangerous man.'

'I'll be careful,' I assured him.

'You must have known he's a gangster.'

'Sure I did, but I wasn't going to let on, was I? He's also a councillor and a big wheel on the city management team.'

'I'll put the kettle on,' Malik said. 'How much are you going to charge him?'

'That's all arranged. He made an offer, I accepted.'

The two of us had been in business together less than a year and already we had taken several grand out of the account. In fact, most money never went into the account in the first place. We don't want to reach the VAT threshold. Almost twelve months but it seemed like yesterday.

Originally, I had set up office in the city centre, near the railway station and the general post office, as a private detective, investigator, debt collector. Rates sky high, although the office was a grotty place up stairs in an old Victorian building that so far has escaped the modernisers. Business was poor; business was non-existent. I would have difficulty paying the rent that month to Burnham, the owner of the block. I was thinking of looking for paid employment.

Then one morning there was a knock on the door. I had wanted it to be a glorious blonde with more money than sense. The kind you sometimes saw in those late-night movies. Mary Astor, for preference, but Jayne Mansfield would do, except she'd been dead all these years, decapitated in a car accident.

No Mary, no Jayne, not blonde. Not even a woman.

'Mr. Rubin?' the man asked.

He was a short fat guy, with dark skin. He could have passed for anything from the Mediterranean area, Levantine, Turkish, Gippo, Tunisian. Turned out he was originally from

Punjab but had lived in England since he was a child. Same as me, if you change Punjab to South Africa.

'So, Mr.....'

'Malik,' the fat guy said.

'How can I help, Mr. Malik?'

The guy didn't exactly look affluent but that didn't worry me. You can never judge money from first appearances. Some of the best suits hide penury.

'Are you alone here?'

Nosy bastard, I thought.

'My associates start later.'

There were no associates, not even a receptionist, but it did not hurt to keep up appearances. The receptionist I had initially employed, a bird aged about seventeen, nice enough, a Methodist, had had to go. What with her wages and the national insurance, and the fact that she knew very little, these were reasons enough. I had shagged her once and that was enough. She had as much animation as a log, though she had held on to my arse during the short strokes, and dug her fingernails into my flesh, the little cow.

'I need a job,' Malik said.

That took me by surprise. Being offered a business opportunity I could not refuse. Being asked to use my office as a drugs outlet. Can you employ my little sister Fatima as your office assistant? But the fat guy seeking a job for himself, that surprised me.

The sad look on Malik's face was almost comical. He looked every inch like a bloodhound with drooping jowls. I decided to let him down gently. But let him down nevertheless.

'I'm not looking to employ anybody right now,' I said. 'But if I were, I doubt you'd be suitable. This is a specialized business, and my clients are -'

'I'm used to dealing with white guys,' Malik interrupted.

I smiled. Wise guys, maybe.

'That wasn't the point I was going to make.'

'And…..I'm willing to work for nothing.'

That clinched it.

'Fuck off, Malik. Nobody works free. Cheap yes, free never.'

'Lots of people work free,' Malik said.

'Yeah! Do-gooders. Liberals who don't know Jack Shit. Voluntary workers. People who attend churches.'

I stood up. The interview, which wasn't an interview, was at an end. Time for Malik to leave. Time for me to make more tea.

'I can put money into the business,' Malik said.

That stopped me in my tracks.

'What makes you think that…?'

'Five thousand, for starters.'

'Pounds sterling or rupees?' I sneered.

'Not shekels,' Malik said.

I had no immediate answer to that. This Malik was sharper than I'd guessed.

'Sit down, Mr. Malik,' I said, and then noticed that Malik had not stood up. 'Cup of tea?'

Two hours later we had made an agreement, and by the end of that first week, with new business, had six thousand quid to deposit in the hitherto ailing account of Rubin & Associates.

'I still don't like it,' Malik said.

'You like money, don't you?'

'Cross him, and he'll…….'

Malik was not sure what Gledhill would do, if he were crossed by anyone.

'Drop me in the canal with concrete boots?'

'Could be.'

'Arrange my…..suicide?'

'He's a nasty piece of work,' Malik said. 'When he goes to the races, he always has a bodyguard. And at the cock-fighting. And the dogs.'

'Dogs? There's no track for a hundred miles of here,' I said.

'Not greyhounds. Dog fighting,' Malik said. 'Up on the moors somewhere, I've heard.'

'Who from?' I asked.

'Khansie.'

Malik had mentioned Khansie several times. If you wanted anything, particularly electrical, top quality, lowest prices, Khansie was your man, according to Malik. There had been the little matter of the new computer. I suggested it one day and the following morning Malik had puffed his way up the steps to the office on the first floor, carrying a computer. Nice job, lots of memory, slim-line screen – and all the records of a local junior school. I had ordered Malik to get the machine out of the office immediately, return it to Khansie. It transpired that Khansie didn't do jobs himself but paid others, young silly buggers desperate for the price of a line, to nick the items. No stock at home; Khansie only set up jobs on demand. In any case the police weren't interested. Well, I was interested. I had not demanded stolen goods and that was that.

Malik asked me one day if I'd like to meet Khansie. I declined. I'd as much interest in meeting this cheap thief as I had in meeting Heinrich ('I like to play a record of Beethoven's music after a busy day in the office') fucking Himmler.

'Never trust gossip and rumour,' I told Malik.

'There's no smoke without fire.'

I covered my face with my hands.

'I fucking knew, just knew, you were going to say that,' I said. 'You and your fucking clichés.'

'The police can't get near Gledhill. He has councillors in his pocket -'

'He is a councillor himself,' I said. 'A member of the cabinet. Which explains why he received permission to build a hotel restaurant and car park on a prime site,' I said. 'I must find out which councillors. Do you know?'

'No.' Malik shook his head.

'Khansie will know,' I said, grinning.

'Now you're taking the mickey, Mr Rubin' Malik said dolefully.

We both drank tea in silence. We had an agreement. Two agreements, in fact. First, we always made our own tea. Second, we never discussed religion. On most other things we agreed, usually, but now Malik was concerned for my safety. He knew his colleague was tough, had seen him in action; knew he was fearless to the point of foolishness; and envied his success with the ladies.

'What's she like?' Malik asked.

'The lovely Wanda?'

'Who else?'

'Well,' I said, 'you could mean the bird I shagged out back at the Telos Club, after Gledhill and the lovely Wanda left.'

I'd been determined to get my end away. When Gledhill had finally decided to leave the public bar and move to a Manchester casino, taking Wanda with him, I had declined the offer to accompany them. There were guys waiting to escort Gledhill; they were paid for that kind of work. I was happy enough to act as protector and guide for the girl friend, the bit on the side, but no way was I going to be one of Gledhill's henchmen.

I'd been about to leave myself but first needed to empty my bladder. The rock shandies had wasted no time passing through to my kidneys. As I came out of the gents, a young bird bumped into me on the corridor. Accidentally on purpose. She was not exactly drunk but she was definitely the worse for wear. In other circumstances I would not have bothered but the evening was passing quickly and I had no wish to pay the cover charges to get into the Club – I had met Gledhill in the public bar area - so it had to be this daft little bird. At first I thought of taking her into the gents, with her bending over the toilet seat in a cubicle – that'd be nostalgie pour la boue and no fucking mistake - but the toilets were well patronised and I didn't fancy the smell of stale urine in there.

'D'you wanna buy me a drink?' she slurred.

The girl was wearing only a skimpy short dress. Her arms and shoulders were bare, and as it was getting late, I supposed she must be cold, but her skin was warm enough when I took her in my arms and kissed her. I ran my fingers across her bare shoulders. Keeping the pot warm.

'You're a lovely girl,' I said. 'Let's go outside.'

'You got a car?'

'Yes, but I left it at home.'

'Why? Cos you wanted to drink?'

'No, because I'm fucking stupid,' I replied.

She burst out laughing, and I pretended to join in but inwardly I was cursing myself. With that car we could have found a quiet spot down near the river or the canal, door wide open, her spread out on the back seat, a cool summer breeze fanning my bare arse. Bang, bang, thank you, ma'am. But now it would have to be out back, somewhere among the dustbins and the crates of empty bottles and the stink of rotten or rotting vegetables. I do not like knee tremblers in back yards but there are occasions when that's what is available and when you're hungry you don't refuse a crust.

'So what happened?' Malik asked, a shiver of vicarious pleasure in his voice.

'I stood her against a dustbin – you know, one of those wheelie bins – and took her from behind. Three or four strokes and she came like a fucking tsunami wave.'

'What about the.....cr.....you know.'

'French letter?'

'Yes,' Malik nodded, excitement in his eyes.

'Took her bareback,' I said. 'But I'd nothing to fear. She was a virgin.'

That wasn't exactly true, not in all particulars. Little girl, she of the skimpy dress, the nice knockers, white knickers, whose age I had not asked, most assuredly was not a virgin.

'Stick to girls like her, Mr Rubin,' Malik said seriously, even sombrely. 'This Wanda tart – she's going to be trouble. I can tell. Real trouble.'

'But she's a dish,' I said. 'Switch on the kettle, will you?' I paused, while Malik flicked the electric switch on the Morphy Richards. 'You want to see her legs.'

'Good, are they?'

'Long,' I said, using my hands to underline the length.

'Long,' Malik repeated, and swallowed hard.

'All the way from her ankles to her arse. And her tits. You should see them. Or perhaps not. The excitement would kill you.'

'Well,' Malik persisted, 'nice tits or not, I still don't like it. You're walking into danger. You're going to come a......'

'Cropper? Come a cropper?'

'It isn't funny,' Malik said.

I made myself a cup of camomile tea, while Malik had what he, and everyone else, calls English tea, but which isn't English at all.

'So, Malik, I think asking Cllr. Gledhill fifty an hour, cash, is fair enough, don't you? He seemed to like it and we shook hands before he departed for the fleshpots of Manchester.'

I'd had to use my left hand, of course.

Chapter Twelve

The flat was in the city centre, close to the riverside.

I pushed the button.

'Hi, Rubin' Wanda said. 'It looks cold out there.'

She could not only hear my voice but see me too.

'Then open this fucking door,' I said.

I could have used the lift but preferred to run up the steps. It is a way of keeping fit without the grind, sweat and boredom of the gym.

On the top floor there was only the one flat, the penthouse. I walked to the front door and knocked.

'It's open,' Wanda called.

I did not move.

The door was eventually opened by Wanda. She was wearing a light pink dressing gown. Some women suit robes.

'I told you it was unlocked.'

'So you did,' I replied.

'So why didn't you come in?'

'Because I'm an awkward sod,' I said.

Without her high-heeled boots, and wearing flat slip-ons, Wanda didn't seem as tall, but she was no dwarf either.

I followed her into the flat, into a spacious sitting room with a large picture window. The view over the south side of the city, with the river, canal and railway line clear in the cloudless morning, pleased me.

Music, something contemporary, influenced by rap or hip-hop, issued from a stack in the corner.

'This must cost Harry Gledhill an arm and a leg,' I said.

'He owns the whole building,' Wanda said.

'And the loudspeakers, the TV, the DVD and all that.....that machinery?'

'Harry's,' Wanda said. 'Coffee?'

I declined. I drink only one cup of coffee a day, always with my breakfast of oats porridge early in the morning.

'Have you any orange juice?'

'I've got everything,' she said. 'The fucking fridge is groaning.'

'Don't swear!' I snapped.

Wanda's face showed her surprise.

'I don't like women who cuss,' I said. 'Especially not a woman of mine.'

'Am I your......woman?'

'No. You're Harry Gledhill's. But he's paying me to take care of you.'

She went to the kitchen, returned with my orange juice.

'Don't you want something to eat?'

'I had breakfast at seven this morning,' I said.

'So early?' she shivered.

'I like the early mornings. But don't let me –'

'I never eat breakfast,' she said.

I shrugged. Turned and looked out of the window again.

'Someone once referred to this as a handsome town,' I said. 'And it was. Until they started to develop it. People like your Henry 'Happy Harry' Gledhill. Show them a solid Victorian building, and they'll fucking pull it down and put concrete blocks in its place. Now, it's about as handsome as my arse.'

'You have a nice arse,' Wanda said, smiling. 'Women like a man with a good arse. There are too many men whose trousers don't fit right.'

I knew the type: slack-arsed mother's boys, sociology lecturers, loblolly men, losers.

I sat down in an easy chair. Wanda sat opposite, legs curled beneath her, on a settee. She had good knees. I notice knees. A good pair of pins are often marred by poor knees. Wanda could see me staring and pretended to cover herself with the robe.

I drank all the orange juice. She asked if I wanted more. I said one glass was enough.

'Right,' I said, and cleared my throat 'To business. Enough of this skating along on the surface.'

On Wanda's face there was a lack of understanding.

'Concrete blocks. Nice arses. Do you want more orange juice? Superficial. Skating the surface. But I'm here because your Harry's paying me. By the hour. And I intend to earn every penny.'

'Coo!' she said, in a childish voice, 'Isn't he forceful?'

'I want to begin by asking you some questions,' I said. 'About yourself. Your interests.'

'Like a career's interview, you mean?'

'I think, Wanda, you've already found your place. That should be OK till you're about forty.'

'Forty?'

'When you're no longer a sexy babe with good tits and shapely legs.'

'Is that what I am now? Sexy with good tits and-'

'Knock it off, Wanda,' I interrupted. 'And turn that fucking noise off, will you?'

'Fuck you!' she said, but she turned off the music nevertheless. 'Fuck you, Rubin.'

I stood up. My fists were bunched.

Wanda shook her head slowly.

'Harry wouldn't like it,' she warned. 'His best girl covered in bruises.'

'Just don't……don't tell me to fuck off, then. Understand?'

'Yes, master,' Wanda said, and she smiled.

She had good teeth. Private dentist, maybe, paid for by Harry Gledhill. Her smile would have melted stone. But I am harder than stone, and determined to keep her under control, at least for as long as I was being paid, by the hour, in cash, by Gledhill.

I laid down the ground rules. She went out, she phoned me first. She had visitors, even girl friends, she cleared it with me first. She was careful who she contacted, by phone or email. She said she didn't have email or internet access, had never bothered to learn, and didn't see why she should.

'Good,' I said.

'Anything else?' Wanda asked, sulking. 'Do you wanna know before I go to the bog…..or should that be toilet, Sir?'

'You miss your fucking periods, I want to know,' I said, unsmiling.

'It's OK for you to eff and blind, but not for me. Why's that?'

'Because I'm a man, and you're not,' I told her.

'Do as I say but not as I do. Is that it?'

'You're getting the message, Wanda. Slowly, but you're getting the message.'

'You know, darling,' she said, smiling archly at me in what she probably took to be a seductive manner, 'I don't think you're as tough as you make out.'

'Just don't do anything that makes me disprove that,' I said.

'Coo! Disprove! Where'd you learn to talk like you do?'

'How do I talk?'

'You know.'

'No, I don't know.'

'All posh, like. As if you went to a good school.'

'I did go to a good school,' I told her. 'But we're not here to discuss education. My job is to take care of you for Happy Harry Gledhill. So listen carefully.'

I tried to make her understand that if Happy Harry was willing to pay for protection, then there must a threat. How big that threat was, how real it was, I did not know, and I did not need to know. I did a job, I took the payment, in notes, off the books. No questions, no cheating, no gossip.

'Maybe there isn't a…..a threat,' Wanda said.

She altered her position and sat with both legs outstretched. Yes, I thought, nice gams and good knees. If she let her robe slip open, I was out of there. For that was a promise I had made to myself, and by implication to Malik

'Maybe,' Wanda continued, 'he just wants to keep an eye on me.'

'Why should he want to do that? Because he has reason not to trust you?'

'Because he's a fuck......a bloody control freak. Can I say bloody?'

'No,' I said.

I stood up and went into the kitchen. She followed me. It was, as estate agents say, nicely appointed: plenty of work tops, a double stainless steel sink; no shortage of cupboards. All a bit IKEA, but serviceable, and Wanda probably thought it was top of the range. The cooker and hob were gas, in an attractive green shade, a Rangemaster 110. There was a small dining table, with two chairs, but I guessed that Wanda probably ate in front of the TV, from a tray, and she had already told me she never took breakfast.

'Do much cooking, Wanda?'

'Naw! Always eat out or send out.'

I went to the bedroom. The flat had one bedroom but it was large enough for a double bed, with space to move all round. In the ceiling there was a large mirror.

'What's up above?' I asked.

'Some loft space,' Wanda said.

'Easy access? Is there a ladder?'

'Something pulls down, I think. I never go up there?'

'Does anyone else?'

Wanda shrugged her shoulders, but did not answer.

I led the way back to the sitting room. I went over to the window. The view was splendid. From this height it was possible to tell how the city had developed. The road layout was clear to see and I had to agree that the inner ring road had been a sensible notion, allowing fast movement of traffic.

'This is all very pleasant,' I said.

'Yes.'

'Nicely appointed. All mod cons. Does he give you money regularly, your Mr Gledhill?'

'I get a monthly clothing allowance, as he calls it, but he pays for the food, the lighting, the gas.'

'Telephone?'

'I've only got the mobile, and he pays for that.'

'Contract?'

'I suppose so. I'm never short of credit.'

I sat down again.

'Spoiled. Pampered even. Want for nothing. You're a lucky girl, Wanda.'

'Think so?'

'Do you……do you like Harry Gledhill?'

'What do you mean?'

'Do you love him? Feel affection for him.'

'Should I?'

'Any girl should try to feel something for her sugar daddy.'

'I'm going to have a shower,' Wanda said. 'Wanna join me?'

'Ever had sex in a shower, Wanda?' I said.

I stood up again. Didn't like her standing over me.

'Yes. Have you?'

'Often,' I answered. 'But it isn't what it's cracked up to be, is it?'

'Speak for yourself.'

Wanda let her robe fall to the floor. All she was wearing was a short nightdress, white in a slight shade of pink. It just about covered her arse. Her figure was curvy; there didn't seem to be an extra ounce of flesh on her body. I caught a flash of pubic hair.

'Well?' she asked.

'Well….what?'

'Like what you see?' she said.

'I'd have to be a long-time resident eunuch in a fucking Turkish harem not to like what I see,' I said.

'I don't understand half what you say,' she said

She moved forward and pressed herself against me. Her arms went round my neck, drawing me even closer. She puckered her lips, expecting a kiss. I could feel the firmness of her tits against my chest, and Percy would, if my trousers were off, certainly be standing firm and proud.

'You can take it as a Yes,' I said.

And I disengaged her arms and pushed her away.

Her mouth shaped into a pout, her eyes showed her puzzlement.

'I am here to protect you,' I said, my voice firm and clear. 'That's what Mr Gledhill is paying me for. There'll be no fucking, no hanky panky.'

I retrieved the robe from the wooden floor and threw it over to her.

'So you have your shower. I'm going back to the office.'

She turned. I liked the arse on it. I liked every part of her body.

'Remember,' I said. 'You don't so much as breathe without clearing it with me first. Understand? I'll write down my cell number.'

'What?'

My mobile number.'

She stopped at the door of the bathroom and turned to face me. She nodded, gloomily, showing her disappointment. She understood.

'I'll write my number down,' I said. 'Then I'll let myself out. Do you have a pen?'

'In my handbag. Over there,' Wanda pointed, sulking.

Then she went into the bathroom and banged the door noisily behind her.

I had two pens of my own, but I wanted to see inside the handbag.

Chapter Thirteen

Outside, it was still warm. Ives was waiting for me, grinning.

'You get around, Mr Rubin' he said, grinning.

'Hello, Ives. How's things?'

He held out his hand to shake mine.

'I'm just going to A & E,' I said. 'Got to see about this hand.'

'Bad, is it?' Ives said.

'As if you cared.'

'You fucked up on the job,' Ives said.

'You can't win 'em all,' I said.

'I'll drive you there.'

'What?'

'The infirmary,' Ives said. 'Get in.'

As usual he was driving a low black car, this time an IS 250, just off the Lexus line.

'I prefer to walk, Ives,' I said.

'You're an awkward sod, you know that? An awkward sod. OK, I'll walk with you.'

He left the car where it was, in a residents' only parking area. That was Ives all over. He parked where he wanted. If he got a ticket, he went along to the office, told them it was all a mistake, assured them – as a last resort – that he'd be taking them to court for racial discrimination, and seeking substantial costs. That was enough for a cowed functionary to open the computer and delete the record. The race relations legislation has been a godsend to the likes of Ives.

We were kept waiting for an hour. A & E departments have become busy places. It would help if they refused entry to drunks and druggies, but that isn't on. They would, like every other sub-human chav, shout and scream about their fucking human rights, the stupid bastards. Less penicillin and more Social Darwinism is what we need to improve the health of the nation.

'Nasty,' the doctor said.

'Are you a doctor?' I asked.

'What do you mean by that?' she asked.

'You look so young,' I told her.

'I'm a house person,' she answered, politically correct.

'Is that what we used to call a houseman?'

'An accident, was it?'

'No, the bastard intended to cut me.'

And he had too.

'You are lucky,' she said. 'He could have severed an artery or done damage to nerves.'

'When does the bandage come off?'

'Now,' the quack said. 'One of the nurses will remove it.' She paused. 'But remember, try to keep out of trouble. Avoid people who carry knives.'

Fucking doctors! Always keen to moralise, to give advice that is beyond the sphere of medicine.

Ives was sitting in the café area. He was not eating or drinking. I didn't blame him. Hospital food, whether in the wards or in the cafeteria, is rarely palatable.

'How did you know where I was?' I asked him.

'Malik told me. I went round to your office.'

'Malik has a big mouth,' I said.

'As soon as I told him I had business for you....' Ives said, allowing the sentence to remain unfinished.

'What kind of business, Ives? If it's carrying messages to West Indians -'

'Afro-Caribbean,' Ives interrupted. 'Please.'

'Bastards who carry knives.'

'You go about armed,' Ives said.

'Not all the time,' I replied. 'Only when the occasion demands it.'

'Well, this one does.'

'What?' I asked.

'Demands that you go armed.'

'Come off it, Ives,' I said. 'I'm in business as a PI. Chasing debts. Checking on errant or possibly errant partners. Small time stuff. I'm not a serious gangster like you.'

Ives stood up. All six foot six of him, dressed entirely in black. He looked like a serious young businessman, not at all like a gangster – which is, perhaps, the way that gangsters choose to look, these days. Ives makes a pretty penny from drugs and prostitution. His powers of organisation must be good. If he had turned his talents to legitimate business, he might have done just was well, perhaps even better, and not constantly run the risk of arrest, or disputes with other gangsters like Danny Muggs.

We walked to the main entrance. We had to push our way through quite a crowd: patients in dressing gowns and visitors, all smoking. The car park was full, and cars were being driven round as visitors searched for a spot to park. It isn't cheap to park a motor in such places, and yet they tell us the National Health service is losing money. It is, of course, losing money, that is.

Ives and I had walked there.

'You going back to that apartment?' he asked.

'No. The office.'

'I'll come with you,' Ives said.

'All this time, and you've still not told me what this business it. What you have to offer.'

Ives, being a tall man, had a long stride. I'm not, at five eleven, exactly a dwarf, but I had trouble keeping up with him.

'Slow down, Ives,' I said. 'What's the hurry?'

'Time is money,' he grinned.

It is rare to see Ives smile. He's a serious guy. He probably thinks that to be seen smiling is to be seen showing weakness. In his line of business, weakness can be fatal.

We walked through Greenhead Park. This is a green lung in the middle of the city. Developers such as Harry Gledhill would give their eye teeth to be able to purchase the park, and one day they will succeed.

Little children were playing on swings and roundabouts, guarded by mothers, most of them with a cigarette between their lips, and a few fathers. Council workers cut grass and clipped hedges. And there were people taking the air, or using the park as a short cut into the city centre, as Ives and I were doing.

'So....what's this job that's so secret you cannot get round to telling me about it, Ives?'

We were passing a kiosk that sold ice cream and lollipops, iced water with colouring, not worth the price being asked.

'Fancy an ice cream?' Ives asked.

I shook my head.

'Me neither,' he said.

I stopped. Looked over at a paddling pool, in which there was no water. The water was being changed by two men wearing bright yellow jackets. They must have been sweating cobs. Something to do with Elf 'n' Safety, I thought.

'You're usually decisive, Ives,' I said. 'So this must be something dangerous or illegal.'

'Both,' he said.

He turned, about to continue walking.

'Stop, Ives!' I commanded. He stopped. 'Don't fucking move! Not until you've told me -'

'Mr Rubin! If anyone else spoke to me as you do, I'd yank their heads off.'

That was what Harry Gledhill had said, in the Telos Bar and Club, but not in exactly those words.

'We need to go somewhere quiet,' Ives said.

As we were standing at the side of a busy road, I was not going to argue.

'Sparrow Park,' I said. 'Do you know it?'

Ives shook his head.

We walked round the corner to what until a few years ago had been a quiet spot where local people met and talked. There had been grass and a couple of benches. Now there was concrete and no benches; just a small brick wall, and it was there that we sat down, opposite a Punjabi supermarket which was hardly big enough to justify the name.

'Face this way,' Ives said.

'Why?'

'There's a camera on the roof.'

'They cannot hear us?'

'Wanna bet? The bastards employ lip readers.'

I smiled. 'So ... let's hear it, Ives.'

How'd you like to earn some easy money, Mr Rubin?'

I shook my head. There is no such thing as easy money. Just as there's no free luncheon. Someone, somewhere, along the line, is paying. One guy's free luncheon voucher is another guy's tax increase.

'Spit it out,' I said.

'Five grand.'

'For what, my tall black friend?'

Ives shrugged his shoulders.

'For very little. A small job, but crucial.'

'Yes.'

'Look out and driver.'

'What are you planning, Ives? A fucking bank heist?'

He winced, almost looked offended.

He shook his head. 'Bank jobs? You must be joking. All that security. And when you get the notes, they have dye all over 'em.'

'A post office?'

'I've hit post offices, small ones. But not recently.'

You know, Ives, getting information out of you today. I'd be easier pushing butter up a donkey's arse using a red hot knitting needle.'

'Me and a few pals are going to hit Danny Muggs. And as - "Hold on, hold on!' I interrupted.

'Well, as he cut you, I thought -'

'When you say you are going to hit him -'

'Me and a few pals.'

'You mean kill him, don't you?'

Ives took hold of my arm and said, speaking softly: 'Mr Rubin I'm into some pretty deep shit, as you know. Girls and dope. I lean on people. I sometimes have to beat a bit of sense into their stupid thick skulls.' I looked at the knuckles on his right hand, and, sure enough, they had seen active service – 'but murder? No!'

'OK! You're just going to rough him up a bit.'

'You got it,' Ives said.

'Rearrange his face,' I said.

'Punishment. Teach him a lesson. Make sure he keeps off my patch. Stops cutting my boys. Like he did you, Mr Rubin.'

'I'm not one of your boys, Ives. Let's be clear about that, shall we?'

In the distance we heard the sound of a klaxon. It could have been the cops or an ambulance. These two services, as they now like to be called, produce a lot of noise pollution in cities. The sound went away on the Doppler effect.

'So what do you say, Mr Rubin?'

'Five grand, to drive the motor, and keep a look out. And Danny gets roughed up but not killed. Is that right?'

Ives smiled broadly.

'So you'll do it?'

'I'll do it.'

Five grand for one day's work. At such a rate I would be tempted to kill Danny Muggs myself.

Chapter Fourteen

'If I don't get out, I'll go crazy,' Wanda said.

'If we're seen around, Harry won't like it,' I said.

I went to the fridge and took out a bottle of 7 Up. I rubbed the cool bottle against my right hand. As the quack at the hospital had said, I was fortunate Danny Muggs hadn't severed a nerve or an important tendon.

'Maybe Harry'll like that. Take away his wife's suspicions.'

'As if he cares,' I said.

'Oh, he cares,' Wanda replied seriously. 'He's shit-scared of his old lady, frightened she'll find out.'

'Hard man like Happy Harry. Scared?'

She nodded, looked unhappy. Tried the TV, found nothing, switched off again.

'Nothing but shit,' she said.

She switched on a music disc. Theme from Exodus, an old movie long forgotten but, as they say, the melody lingers on. My mother enjoyed the movie, made her cry. But then, so did most movies, make her cry, I mean.

Wanda was a handsome woman, with flesh on her, not fat, not a stick insect either. Sure, I fancied her, but I'd made my vow of abstinence, and that was that.

'Why you doin' this, Rubin?'

'Looking after you, for Harry?'

'Yeah.'

'The money,' I said.

She paced the flat, like the caged animal that in reality she was.

'You won't fuck me,' she said, looking at me. 'You won't take me out. What do you want? I can take my clothes off and you can watch.'

'Watch?'

'Me frigging myself,' she said.

'Do you frig yourself often, Wanda?'

'I have to. Harry can't bring me off.'

She swayed seductively. I could feel Percy becoming aroused. The music from Exodus was still playing. Wanda was doing some sort of ballet dance, and doing it well. She ended up writhing on the floor. She removed her white panties, fingers explored her quim, and very soon she was panting.

'Knock it off, Wanda!' I barked harshly.

She sat up, smiled cockily.

'What? Didn't you like it? Harry enjoys watching me frig myself.'

'Can he tell when you fake it?'

'I always fake it,' she said. There was a look of sadness in her eyes. I've seen that look many times. In most cases it's as fake as the orgasm. 'No man's made me come to orgasm, ever. And I was fucked at the age of fourteen.'

'Never?'

'Never,' she said, sitting cross-legged.

'And who was the peasant who first tupped you?'

'I worked Saturdays at a Greek Restaurant. The owner was a fat, middle-aged Greek. He raped me in the back.'

'Raped?'

'Well, not raped. I was up for it. He stunk of garlic and olive oil.'

I did not respond. There are more important ills in the world than a bird being shagged by a Greek, or a woman who can't reach orgasm.

'You don't care, do you, Rubin?'

I shook my head. 'No.'

'Not even a bit?'

'I don't give a monkey's toss,' I said.

Now she shook her head, but in disbelief.

'Do you care about anything? Anybody?'

I pretended to ponder the question, then said, 'No, I can't think that I do.'

She put on her knickers. Percy became quiescent again.

'Another 7?' she asked.

I nodded. I thought 7 Up was a drink, until I read Snow White.

She returned with the soft drink.

'Fancy a Chinese?' Wanda asked.

'If she's female, I might.'

She rang for two takeaways.

'Mr Rubin?' She was sitting on the sofa opposite me. Her voice was serious, plaintive even.

'Yes.'

'I'm bored. Bored out of my skull. And I'm not getting any younger.'

'Welcome to the human race.'

'What's the meaning of life, Mr Rubin? Do you ever wonder? Why we are here. What's the purpose of it all?'

'I'll tell you, Wanda. I used to wonder about it a lot. Now I don't think about it. When I'm tired, I sleep. When I'm hungry, I eat? When I awake, I get up.'

'And when you get horny?' she smiled.

The doorbell rang.

'That didn't take him long,' I said.

'Go get it. I'll set the plates and cutlery.'

'Open this bloody door,' a harsh voice commanded.

It wasn't the Chinese takeaway man. It was Councillor Henry Happy Harry Gledhill.

Harry was flushed and sweating.

He saw me and removed his shades. On him there was the smell of cigar smoke.

'The bloody lift. It's out of order.'

'Again,' Wanda added.

'Where can a man find some proper bloody service?'

'Try Gawthorne Holdings,' I said.

Harry treated me to a murderous stare but said nothing.

'Are you alone?' I asked.

'Why shouldn't I be?' Harry snapped.

'You often have muscle in attendance,' I said.

Harry smile briefly.

'I amuse you, Councillor Gledhill?'

'It's the way you talk sometimes. If I didn't know better, I'd say you were a ponce.'

The door bell sounded. Wanda checked. It was the takeaway guy. Wanda unlocked the outer door, so the guy could labour his way up the steps.

We shared the two meals three ways. Wanda ate like a horse that hasn't been fed and watered for at least three weeks. I ate as much as her, but more slowly. I used my fingers a lot; that is how I like to eat. Harry ate very little: no doubt he had eaten already, a homely meal prepared by 'er indoors.

Conversation did not come easily. We did not have enough in common for that. Harry was bright enough in his own way but we belonged to different backgrounds, different generations, and Wanda, though she was a cute kid, nice figure and all that, was not as well endowed in her brain as in her body.

Once or twice Harry Gledhill seemed to be on the point of saying something, suggesting something, but if he were, he drew back at the last minute. What this something might be, I could not begin to guess. But I was soon to learn.

Wanda cleared the dishes. I went to the bathroom to wash my hands. When I returned to the sitting room, I came to the conclusion that I had interrupted a conversation. Both had been talking, but now they clammed up.

I did not sit down.

'I came round to be sure that Wanda was OK,' I said.

'That's what I'm paying you for, Jack.'

'Yes, but now that you're here, Harry, Wanda is in good hands. And I don't want to play gooseberry.'

'No, don't leave,' Harry Gledhill said hastily. 'I...er...I have a proposition for you.'

It was my day for propositions. First Ives, and now Harry Gledhill. The bank balance of Rubin & Associates was, at last, in rude health.

I waited for him to tell me what the proposition was. I could see him fidgeting, being indecisive. This from a man who was a member of the city council, a leading light of the cabinet, a decision maker on behalf of hundreds of thousands of people.

Wanda broke the silence.

'Harry?'

Her voice was timid.

'Yes.'

'Can I have smoke?' Wanda asked.

That puzzled me for a moment.

Harry looked dubious.

'I hear that you are discreet,' Harry said.

'Whatever Wanda does, goes with me to the grave,' I said.

What with the simmering tension in that room, and the poor quality of the conversation, the grave was beginning to seem less forbidding than formerly.

Wanda fairly scampered out of the room and into her bedroom.

'Marijuana?' I asked.

'To begin with,' Harry said. 'And if that doesn't turn her on. Something.....'

'A little stronger?'

'You've got it.'

'Do you partake, Harry?' I asked.

'Me?'

'No, that little yellow man hiding under the table,' I said with a sneer. Harry actually clocked the table. 'Who else could I possibly mean?'

'Never touch the stuff,' Harry told me. 'Nothing stronger than beer, or the occasional short. You?'

I shook my head.

'There are better ways of getting high, Harry.'

'How do you get high, Mr Rubin?'

He seemed to be genuine in his enquiry.

'There are many ways,' I said. 'But a good poem does it for me.'

'Poetry? You're pulling my pisser.'

'You should be so lucky, Harry,' I said, and laughed.

It seemed to take Wanda an inordinate amount of time to smoke her joint. I began to wonder if she might be injecting. I hadn't noticed any puncture marks in the superficial veins of her arms, and would surely have done so.

Finally, the bedroom door opened. Wanda adopted pose. We were meant to take notice of what she was wearing, or, rather, not quite wearing. She had on a pink bra and a pair of pants. The large pants currently in fashion; only chavs favour thongs nowadays, or so I have been reliably informed.

'It's Showtime,' Wanda announced, and started to giggle.

She was somewhat unsteady on her feet. This and the giggling persuaded me she had taken something rather stronger than marijuana. She successfully made her way to the music centre and played the music she had listened to earlier, the theme from the movie Exodus. Although a keen watcher of movies, this is one I have never seen. I told you, it was one of my mother's favourites. It made her weep. But then, she was a lachrymose person and wept a lot. The old girl had a lot to be lachrymose about.

Wanda started to dance, the sort of ballet moves she had shown me earlier, before the arrival of harry Gledhill. Unlike the earlier performance, however, she now added a number of other interesting moves. Slowly, provocatively, she removed her bra. Free at last, her breasts seemed to rejoice. Wanda had nice tits, no doubt about that. She stroked them, pulled on the nipples, cupped them in her hands and held them close to Harry and then to me. I could smell perfume that she had applied while in the bedroom.

I looked across at Harry Gledhill. He was staring intently, rapt by Wanda's beauty.

Next, Wanda stroked her belly and her thighs, her fingers moving ever closer to her private parts, soon, no doubt, to surrender whatever secrets they held.

Harry removed his tie. His face was red and sweating. This guy was a grade A candidate for a stroke or even a heart attack. If he suffered a heart attack, too bad: he would not get the kiss of life from me. Not only was he much too ugly, but he was also a man, and in any case I did not favour his political opinions.

Slowly, slowly and with intent, Wanda began to roll down her knickers. Keeping her movements in synch with the music. The music that had been written for a story of Jews escaping from Europe in search of a better life in the land of their forefathers. And now being debased by this bird who could not dance well, but who pleased the older man sweating in his chair.

Completely naked now, Wanda came up close to me and pushed her pudenda into my face. I tried to remain composed.

'Come on, Rubin' she pleaded.

I looked across at Harry.

'Take her, Rubin' he urged, his voice hoarse. 'Take her.'

I gently pushed Wanda to one side and stood up. She reached out to unfasten the belt supporting my trousers. I pushed her away, rougher this time.

'She's yours for the taking,' Harry Gledhill said, his voice as dry as a donkey's arse, rough and hoarse.

I saw that the zip, on Harry's trousers was undone. The message was clear.

I strode over to the music centre and switched off. Wanda stopped gyrating.

'Wanda,' Harry said, 'get me a drink of water.'

Harry drank gratefully.

'You don't know what you're missing, Mr Rubin' he said, his voice clearer now.

'Oh, yes, I think I do,' I replied. 'And I know why you put me on a retainer. I shag Wanda while you watch. And, judging by your open zip' – Harry hastily fastened the zip – 'you were going to watch and have a wank.'

He averted his eyes.

'Get your fucking clothes on, Wanda,' I said.

She disappeared into the bedroom.

'How much do I owe you?' Harry Gledhill enquired savagely, taking out his wad.

'Fuck all,' I said.

I wondered later if I would have been so cavalier in my refusal had I not been going to pick up five grand for one day's work with Ives.

I moved to the door. Stopped, turned.

'It's not too late, Wanda. My advice – take it or leave it – is cut yourself off from this fucking pervert. Don't wait till tomorrow. Get out tonight. Go home to your parents. Stay in a hostel for battered women. Book a room in the Station Hotel. But get out.'

Sometimes I surprise myself.

Chapter Fifteen

'I don't believe you,' Malik said, his brown eyes wide open.

'Well you had better,' I said, 'because it's all true.'

'I do believe you,' Malik added. 'What I find difficult is that you were able – it was there, right in front of your nose, and -'

'All I had to do was put my tongue out and I'd have touched it,'I said. 'The pulse of desire.'

'I couldn't have done it,' Malik said. 'Turn it down, I mean.'

'Would you have been comfortable with Gledhill tossing himself off while you were trying to give Wanda a good seeing to?'

'I wouldn't even have noticed him,' Malik said, and he grinned.

Malik grinned a lot but rarely smiled. Probably didn't want to expose his stained teeth. His breath wasn't always as fresh as it ought to have been, which may have been because in his house it was curry with everything.

There was a knock on the door. Malik straightened his tie, in anticipation of a customer for Rubin Associates. He licked his lips and strode purposefully to the door.

I heard a female voice.

'Come in,' Malik said.

The girl stood there.

'I never expected to see you again,' I said.

Malik stood behind the girl, a lascivious gleam in his eyes.

The last time we had met she had been wearing a skimpy dress and carried only a handbag. Now she had on the same skimpy dress, or something similar, but was carrying a black plastic bag, the kind used as a bin liner, or, as in this case, a girl's worldly goods.

'Young Jennifer,' I said. 'Sit down. You look worn out.'

'Would you like a cup of tea or coffee?' Malik asked, anxious to be in on the act.

'Never drink coffee,' she said.

'Tea, then?'

'Never drink tea, either.'

'Give her a glass of water,' I told him.

Bedar put on the kettle. To make a drink for himself. He knows better than to make anything for me. When we first started working together, I insisted on a simple rule: I make my own tea and coffee, the way I like it; and there must be no discussion of religion – no way.

Able to look closely at Jennifer, I could see that she was indeed worn out, had been experiencing a bad time. I looked for signs of bruising on her arms and legs, but there were none.

'What happened, Jenn? Ives put you to work?'

'He suggested it. But I wasn't having it.'

'Did he shag you?' I asked.

Malik winced. He can never get used to the way I talk to women.

That was the way with pimps and whore masters: shag a girl regularly, say that he loved her to the exclusion of all others, and get her hooked on drugs. Then out working, which in Ives' case meant, as far as I knew, the streets and clubs of the city of Nottingham.

'Not once,' she said.

'For fuck's sake, Malik! Where is the girl's water.'

Malik had forgotten. He was too busy looking down the front of Jennifer's dress, getting an eyeful of her bra-less boobs.

'Did he beat you?'

She shook her head.

'Then what happened? You look as if you haven't slept for at least a week.'

'Been livin' rough, aint I?'

'I think, my dear, you'd better stay at my place tonight.'

Malik leered and made an obscene gesture behind the girl's back.

'Wha'ever,' she said, shrugging her slim shoulders.

She sat beside me in the car going home, her eyes shut, and she may well have been asleep, such was the shroud of silence that enveloped her. I sighed. What an idiot I was, taking this girl home, when the chances were slim that we would enjoy sex again, as we had in the hotel in Cambridge. On that occasion I had never asked her where she was going, standing at the side of the road hitching a lift, and not much caring where the lift took her. Whatever her reasons, they were her own. Where women are concerned, I do not ask too many questions; and they had not try to question me too closely, not unless they wanted a smack in the mouth.

On arrival at my place, an old farmhouse on the side of the Pennine hills, it was necessary to rouse her.

'Jennifer!'

'My answer was a snore.

Snores are passion killers at the best of times, and this was not the best of times.

I dug my elbow into her body.

'What the fuck....?'

'Don't curse,' I said.

I had to help her to get out of the car and to the door of the house. I leaned her against a wall while I took out my house keys and by the time I'd opened the door she had slid down the wall. It was as if she were drunk, or under the influence of drugs.

I filled my lungs with fresh air and picked her up. I deposited her on the settee in the sitting room. She opened her eyes.

'Rubin!' she said.

'So you remember something.'

'Aren't you going to ask where I've been?'

'No,' I said. 'I don't want to know, and I don't care.'

'Fuck you!' she said.

I took her by shoulders and shook her roughly.

'Don't you ever say that to me again. Hear me?' And added, quite unnecessarily: 'You fucking little slag.'

'You swear. Why can't I?'

'I'm a man, and you're not.'

'Some reason.'

'And because this is my house, my place. I pay the mortgage. And that gives me the right to make the rules.'

She sat there. She sulked. That was better than listening to her snore.

'Are you hungry?'

'I'm tired,' she said.

'That isn't what I asked you, Jennifer.'

'Do you know, Rubin? You bore me stiff.'

There was a coldness in her voice. I concluded that I did not like her, not in this mood, and I was not going to hang around waiting for her to show me other sides of her character. No woman has ever told me that I bored them. I may have done, but they have never told me.

'Well, are you hungry, or are you not?'

She repeated what I had asked, mimicking my voice, and not doing it well.

'I'll cook for both of us,' I said.

'What are you going to make?'

'It'll be a surprise, girl. And let me tell you this: you'll eat it, if I have to ram it down your fucking throat.'

'You make me fucking sick,' she said.

I smacked her hard across the face. She fell back, hit the wall.

'One more remark like that, and I'll tear your fucking head off.'

'Get off my back,' she spat at me. 'Keep out of my hair.'

I grabbed her by the arms and lifted her up from the floor.

Again she spat at me and this time the saliva landed and stuck to my face. I wiped it off with my sleeve. Grabbed her again and put her across my knee on the settee. She struggled. I tanned her arse.

I let her go. She looked round the room.

'No fucking cushions?' she asked.

'What do you want a cushion for?'

I never buy cushions. If I ever need to sleep on the settee, I can always bring a couple of pillows from the bedroom. Truth is, I never need to sleep on the settee or in an easy chair.

She saw the books in my bookcase.

There was a wicked look in her eyes.

'Touch those and you die,' I said.

She read a couple of titles but did not actually touch a book.

'A History of Western Philosophy by ….....'

'Bertrand Russell,' I said.

'The London Book of.....poncy poetry,' she said scornfully.

I was about to inform her that reading poetry is a man's interest, and any remarks about being a poufter were out of place and out of order, but I did not even have time to begin. Jennifer grabbed both books and threw them at me. I managed to grab hold of both before they fell on to the floor and lost some of their pages. Those are two books I have had for a long time – I inherited them, you might say – and I care more about them, and my other volumes, than any human being I know, or am likely to know.

I put both books down carefully. I smiled at the girl. On her face there was a look of triumph. She knew she'd upset me. I could expect her to chuck more books about. I smiled in order to disarm her. It worked. I could see her relax. And as soon as I did, I strode fast across the room and socked her on the jaw. Not the kind of blow I'd administer to a man, but enough to fell her.

I knelt beside her and tore at her dress. She did not resist. I removed her panties. I noticed that they appeared to be of good quality. Not from Primark, I'd warrant.

I removed my own clothing. I straddled her. She spat again and scored another hit. I didn't even bother to wipe off the saliva.

We fought and writhed, there on the floor of the sitting room. I took her from the front; I took her doggy fashion. She bit and scratched and clearly enjoyed every second of it.

She came with a scream of pleasure, digging her finger nails into my buttocks and when it was my turn, shortly afterwards, it was like a roar of fierce wind in a tunnel.

'Jesus, Rubin!' she said, still moaning, her naked body lathered in sweat. 'You sure know how to fuck.'

I stood up.

'First, we take a shower,' I said, ' and then I cook a meal.'

She smiled.

'I take it I'm being invited to stay the night.'

133

'If you behave yourself.'

While I was boiling rice and opening a tin of processed peas, and cutting slices of cold pork, Jennifer came into the kitchen.

'Don't you want to know?'

'No.'

'I mean, what happened when you let me go with Mr Ives.'

'Not interested,' I said.

'You're a cold bastard, aren't you?'

'If you like.'

I'm tired,' she said, suppressing a yawn. 'After the nosh, it'll be straight to sleep for me.'

'That's OK by me.'

'What will you do, Rubin?'

I shrugged my shoulders. I would do what I always do. Read a book in bed. For some reason, I fancied a volume of poetry by W B Yeats. I'd had enough of the pleasures of the flesh. I needed something to feed the mind.

Chapter Sixteen

I ought to have been suspicious. Five grand, just to act as look-out and driver. But how was I to know what the going rate was among gangsters?

Malik, ever a doom-sayer, warned me against having anything to do with Ives's plan for revenge, if in fact it were revenge. It wasn't that what I was planning to do probably involved illegal activity. He had no objections to growing cannabis or to cheating on the benefits' system. He, like a lot of his brethren, had been doing this for many years. Nor was it because he liked me or admired me; what is there to like or admire? I think his real reason was that he saw me as a useful idiot; someone who could use his intelligence to keep him in business. Sure, he had put five grand into the business the same day that we met, but I had no illusions: he had made enquiries, had sussed me out beforehand, and had concluded that I was a safe bet to quadruple his money in a relatively short time.

We had complementary skills, Malik and I, and he knew it. If I came a cropper in Canning Town, or wherever Ives was going to confront Danny Muggs, he would not be able to continue business in the same successful way. That we had been successful in a short period of time could not be denied. And it had all been legal. I had stressed to Malik that there was a line across which I would not cross, and now, like the pillock I can sometimes be, I was about to cross it, and with a vengeance. So why was I making a fool of myself? It was not the five grand, merely, although that was going to be welcome. But the fact that Danny Muggs had cut me, and would have really carved me up if he had had the chance.

I'd had time to think about it. Yes, I wanted my own revenge. And, as the man said – the one who did certainly not write the plays of Shakespeare - revenge is a kind of wild justice. But there is an even older saying, to the effect that revenge is a dish best eaten cold. Th sweet thing was that Ives was going to exact revenge, and I was to be little more than an observer, and for my trouble I was going to be paid five big ones. It had to be good and it was a chance I wasn't going to pass up.

Before I travelled down to London, I had to drive up north. To the Lake District. It is a journey I make quite often, and not just because of the scenery, though that is worth anybody's time.

A young scholar from Johannesburg was invited to become Rabbi in a small old community situated in a small dorp on the high veldt. On his very first Shabbat, a hot debate erupted among the congregation as as to whether one should or should not stand during the reading of the Ten Commandments.

Next day, the rabbi visited an old woman in the nursing home.

'My dear, I'm asking you as the oldest member of the community,' said the rabbi, 'what is our synagogue's custom during the reading of the Ten Commandments?'

'Why do you ask?'

'Yesterday we read the Ten Commandments. Some people stood, some people sat. The ones standing screamed at the ones sitting, telling them to stand up. The ones sitting screamed at the ones standing, telling them to sit down.'

'That,' said the old woman, 'that is our custom.'

I'd set off early in the morning. I wanted to make good time before the roads became too busy. Like the Rabbi, I was going to see an old woman, but this one was only seventy-four and she does not have all her marbles at home. In fact, she has no marbles at all. Her name is Mrs Rubin.

I took the scenic route, stopped several times to stare at distant views of hills, and on a couple of occasions to stand by quiet rivers and stare. After Kendal, where I did not stop, I was in the Lake District. There was a café offering morning tea and coffee. I went in, ordered camomile tea and a scone with jam, butter and cream. It was not cheap. The waitress gave me a teapot and hot water, and I drank three cups. Not that I felt thirsty. But I was in no hurry to reach the nursing home. Indeed, a part of me never wanted to reach it.

The weather on the way up had been good. Now clouds gathered. I could see the summit of Helvellyn. Soon, with cloud cover, it would not be possible to see that far up. The peak of Helvellyn is the highest on the north-south ridge situated between the Thirlmere valley to the west, and Patterdale to the east. The eastern side of the fell is geographically the most dramatic. I climbed it once, long before my mother was admitted to a home here. Climbed alone, which is always stupid, but, then, good sense has never been my strength. Near the summit is Red Tarn, so named because of the colour of the surrounding screes rather than its water which contains brown trout and fresh-water herring. There used to be lead mining here and the miners took water from the tarn. The summit of Helvellyn is over three thousand feet and I don't give a monkey's what that is in the metric system.

Since my last visit white dividing lines have been painted in the parking area. Rain was falling. In the Lake District the rain hardly ever seems to stop.

I never run through rain. Get your shirt wet, it'll soon dry. Stupid of me, for the rain was falling so heavily that by the time I reached the entrance, I was soaked to the skin.

The door was locked. Don't want the residents wandering away and falling into Thirlmere. Don't want them getting dressed in the middle of the night and trying to go to the open market.

I rang the bell. It was answered by a young woman.

'Oh, you are wet,' she said.

I introduced myself. She allowed me in. Sat me down in a waiting room. Told me I'd have to speak to Matron first. I took off my shirt and hung it over a chair.

'Mr Rubin? Good morning. Or is it afternoon?' Matron said. 'Oh, you are wet, aren't you?'

'It'll be fine soon, Matron.'

We had met before. She seemed to be a sensible woman. She sat down. Stared at me.

'I hope my bare chest doesn't trouble you.'

'I've seen more than a bare chest, Mr Rubin. I'm a nurse, you know.'

'How is my mother?'

'Not too good, I'm afraid.'

'Specifically?'

'She's developing delusions. Seems to think people are against her.'

'Most people are. It isn't a delusion.'

'You don't seriously believe that, do you?'

'Yes, I do.'

'Who are these people?'

'They're called goyim.'

She shook her head. Hadn't a clue what I meant.

'In this country, Matron,' I said, 'most people aren't usually hostile. They just don't care.'

'There's another thing,' she said.

'Yes?'

I put my shirt on. It was still wet and clung to me. It would be the only thing that did on this day.

'Your mother is becoming increasingly incontinent.'

'And you're holding me here while they clean her up.'

'No, Mr Rubin that's not the reason.'

'Then what is?'

'I think I've explained the lay-out before. On your first visit.'

I remembered. There were four units, and as people deteriorated, they were moved along. Units 3 & 4 were on the upstairs level. It was a steady and inevitable progression to death. Just like life itself.

The progressive loss of cognitive function in senile dementia – call it Alzheimer's disease, if you wish - is accompanied by pathological changes in the brain. One of these is the formation of plaques, little pads in the spaces between nerve cells. The plaques are comprised of a brain protein called beta amyloid. Another protein, called tau, which normally channels chemical messages inside nerve cells, collapses into tangles that appear like twisted bits of thread inside nerve cells. As the disease progresses, nerve cells in several brain areas shrink and die, including cells that normally produce critical neuro-transmitters, the chemical messengers that relay brain signals from one nerve cell to another. Acetylcholine is a neuro-transmitter that is deficient in people with Alzheimer's. As nerve cells continue to die, the brain itself shrinks and the fissures along its surface become smoother.

'So you've downgraded my mother. Is that it?'

'Not downgraded, no. It doesn't work like that.'

'Then how does it work?'

'It reflects the fact that as people become progressively more senile, they need closer nursing care.'

'I understand, matron.'

'I'm glad you do,' she said. 'A lot of people become aggressive when they're told. Or they just cry.'

'I don't cry.'

'Was she a good mother, Mr Rubin?'

The past tense, already.

'She was a talker. Strong sense of humour. Like all Jewish mothers, I suppose.' I paused. 'When I came home from school and told her I'd been given a part in a play as a Jewish husband, she told me to tell the teacher I wanted a speaking part.'

Matron smiled.

'Another joke, Mr Rubin?'

'How many Jewish mothers does it take to change a light bulb? Answer: Don't bother, I'll sit in the dark, I don't want to be a nuisance to anybody. When a tramp approached her in the street and told her he hadn't eaten any food for a week, she told him not to bother her with his anorexia.'

'I think we can go through now, Mr Rubin. Is your shirt dry?'

They had placed my mother in a large armchair, with her feet on a footstool. She was wearing a dressing gown and was covered with a light blanket. Her hair had been brushed till it shone.

Hello, Mam.'

She looked at me, imperiously. As a child I saw that imperious stare many times.

'Are you the doctor?'

'It's me, Mam.'

A male nurse or carer came to ask me if I'd like anything to drink.

I said I'd take cold water.

When he returned with a glass, he said,

'You OK now, Mrs Rubin?'

My mother beamed happily. She turned to me and introduced the other guy as her son.

'He's a good boy,' she said.

'I'm thinking of taking a trip to South Africa, Mam.'

'It's a long way, isn't it? South America.'

'South Africa, mam.'

She looked around. Spotted one of the other patients.

'She's no better than she ought to be,' she said with considerable venom.

'Doonesfontein,' I said.

I told her I could afford it, had recently taken a short well-paid job.

She stared toward the light of the window. There was no smile on her face, not even the vacuous grin that often accompanies senility.

A woman walked over to us. Said she was going down to the shops. Did we want anything bringing back? Then walked off without waiting for an answer, which she wouldn't have had in any case.

'Yes,' I said. 'Doonesfontein. In South Africa. A couple of weeks there might do the trick.'

Now she might remember my father, the man she had left twenty years before. Left him, left the country. For South Africa as such she had never had strong ties of emotion. Her country of birth was Lithuania. When he wanted a bride, my father had used the old Litvak network. He'd rescued my mother from Soviet communism and found himself a bride at the same time. It didn't take long for them to conceive a child and within a year I'd been born.

'I've been in better hotels than this one,' my mother said haughtily.

'You owned one, mam,' I said. 'You and dad.'

There was no reaction to that. No sign that memory had been awakened.

After an hour I decided, for all the good I was doing, I might as well leave.

I went to Matron's office.

'Thanks,' I said.

'I know it isn't always easy, Mr Rubin.'

'You were right, she's deteriorating.'

'It's a long way to travel.'

'But worth every minute,' I said. 'Just for the quality of the conversation.'

'You and your jokes, Mr Rubin.'

'Yes, me and my bloody jokes.'

I went out to the car. Let the rain fall on me. Uncaring rain. Looked across to the lake. Gazed up to the summit of Helvellyn, covered in cloud. Never again would I climb that mountain, either stupidly alone or even with a climbing companion.

I took off my shirt. Put on a jersey I'd brought with me in case it turned cooler.

I turned to go along the side of the lake toward the main road south. As I drove I thought of another story. Here's a joke for you. Woman gets a call to go to South Africa. She doesn't know the fellow, never having left Lithuania before, but she's pleased to be escaping at last from a brutal tyranny. She was pleased to be able to marry, and have a child. Relatives were being confined to gulags. Under an earlier tyranny fourteen of the closest members of her family had been murdered in a camp.

When her marriage had foundered, she moved to a safe country, to bring up her child alone, work hard and pay for him to have a decent education. Maybe he'd become a surgeon or a barrister. For some people senility must be a blessing, an escape from the awful tyranny that is life.

Chapter Seventeen

Dawn was breaking as the motor, driven by Ives, left the M1 and hit the north circular. Ives know where he was going. I'd tried to catch some sleep on the way down but had failed. We were soon in the East End somewhere, but I could not have told you where. The weather had been clear all the way south. Now it started to belt down, a remorseless downpour.

It was about now that I entertained the brief thought that all this was a mistake, but it was a fleeting emotion. If we were to be successful I needed to be focussed.

I was wearing a long loose jacket. My gun was in a holster clipped on to my belt. I'd thought long and hard about going tooled up. Ives had insisted. If things went wrong for him, he said, I might need to fight a rearguard action. Good sense demanded I had something to defend myself with. Ives had provided the gun. He'd poured scorn on my Browning and had provided a Colt, and the holster to go with it. He started to talk technical and I switched off. Gun talk is not something that has ever interested me. It's a bit like body building. Smacks of narcissism.

I'd no idea where we were, except at one stage I saw a sign for a café that said Millwall Caff. That meant we were somewhere along the western side of the Isle of Dogs. This was once a dockers' area, a place of mean houses and large families, but much has now been developed. Originally known as Marshwall, its name derives from the large number of windmills built on the river wall in the 19th century.

Ives stopped the car outside a warehouse or some such building. Judging from the broken window and the boards, the place was deserted.

I could feel the tenseness emanating from Ives. This was no everyday, take the Underground to the office kind of job. This was a fight for territory.

The main door of the warehouse was locked with large padlocks and chains. Ives took one look, shook his head, and came back to the car. He opened the car boot and from it took a large black bag. It seemed to be heavy, even for a tough guy like Ives.

'Get behind the wheel, Mr Rubin' he said quietly. 'I'm going round the back. Keep the engine running.'

Two hours I waited, the engine running. The first hour I kept intense watch for Ives. The second hour, I relaxed a little and listened to the car radio. I played soft music.

When Ives finally returned, he was panting a little.

'Took me longer than I thought,' he said, sliding into the passenger seat.

I refrained from asking what it was that had taken him longer than expected.

The time was nine o'clock.

Ives took hold of his cell phone and punched in a number. The person on the other end took his time answering.

'Danny?' Ives said. He paused. 'Get up in the morning, man.'

There was no Caribbean patois.

'I've mined your warehouse with explosive – just listen up, Danny, will you? - and I can activate the timers....'

I could hear Danny Muggs speaking fast but not make out the words.

Ives listened with patience, a smile on his lips.

'You get round here, Danny. Pronto. Alone. Get that? Alone!'

More words and protests from Danny Muggs.

'That's the way it is, Danny,' Ives said, with restraint and coolness. 'We meet, man to man. Nobody else. Any funny moves, I blow the warehouse and your stash sky high.' 'He paused. 'Now. Alone, Danny. OK?'

And he switched off.

I could feel my pulse beginning to race. Maybe Ives was also tensed up; if so, he did not show it.

He got out of the motor and went to the boot. He placed the bag in the boot again. And returned with a pistol and two knives.

The knives were long. Any longer and they'd have been swords, I tell you.

'What the hell kind of weapon is that, Ives?' I asked.

'It's a Glock 18,' he said. 'Police and counter-terrorist unit gun. Not available to civilians.'

'You have one.'

'I have my.......connections,' Ives said, and he smiled grimly. 'This baby fires more than a thousand rounds a minute.'

'That should be enough to finish off Danny Muggs,' I replied sardonically.

'It's not meant to kill him,' Ives said. 'I jus' wanna frighten him.'

'Well, it frightens me.'

'I need it, Mr Rubin,' Ives said with intense seriousness.

'You mean, you don't expect Danny Muggs to come alone?'

'No, I don't! The bastard will come mob-handed,' Ives said. 'Now listen up, and I'll tell you where to park.'

'You wouldn't like to pay me the five grand now, would you? In used notes.'

It was about now that I wished fervently that I'd listened to Malik and had stayed at home.

Then it happened. A van, black, with no windows, arrived at the front of the warehouse. Five men got out and looked warily around. All were black guys. I strained my eyes, because

I was far off, parked where Ives had advised. I thought I could make out Danny Muggs. I couldn't be certain: I'd only seen him once before, and there had been no time to notice his features. But as he was the one giving orders, I assumed – correctly as it turned out – that the little guy must be Danny. Leaders are often little men. Think Napoleon. Think Mussolini. Think of just about any dictatorial bastard that history throws up.

I saw Danny look up at the building. And the reason. Ives was standing at an opening on the third floor where once a window had been.

Suddenly there was a burst of machine gun fire. Ives had treated his opponents to the sound of his Glock 18. More than a thousand rounds a minute. The men all scattered. All save one. Danny Muggs did not move. He guessed that at this stage, Ives had no intention of killing him. What Ives wanted was to parley. To tell Danny to keep his fingers off Nottingham and, possibly, to cede Leicester to him. Or, maybe, suggesting a way they could work together in harmony, for mutual benefit.

The men who had arrived with Danny Muggs had left the scene, and moved to the rear of the building. I wanted to shout to Ives and tell him to mind his back. But it was pointless; Ives would have secured his back, of that I could be certain.

The two men shouted to each other; there was no other way to be heard. Then Danny Muggs also went round to the rear of the building.

I was torn between a number of possible courses of action. To stay where I was, and hope that Ives would emerge unscathed. To go in there and in some way assist Ives, even though he meant nothing to me, was not even a friend. Or to drive away from the scene before the arrival of the cops. Somebody must have heard the burst of gunfire and reported it. Me being me, sometimes foolish, sometimes quixotic, I chose the option that was most dangerous.

I got out of the motor and ran across the open space in front of the warehouse, a space, no doubt, where once there had been workers' houses, now demolished, awaiting development.

There was no one guarding the rear entrance. I listened at the door. I could hear shouting. Nobody had been ordered to be quiet, and thus sneak up on Ives stealthily. Ives didn't stand a chance: five against one. Well, I might try to improve the odds by one.

I moved slowly and carefully. The warehouse was a large open space but filled with crates and boxes. It was quite dark in there, because of the boards against what had been windows. Then there was a burst of gunfire. I froze. Waited. And then moved forward stealthily. I went round the side of a large crate. If that was filled with dope, somebody must be a rich man. That somebody was Danny Muggs. And saw two bodies: one guy dead, lying there still; the other moaning, his body bleeding, about to die. Ives had changed the odds dramatically. Now it was him against Danny and one other. I had no need to be part of the equation.

I leaned against a crate. I was feeling exhausted, dog-tired. I heard a man shout. There was a burst of gunfire. A scream. Then silence.

How long the silence lasted, I could not tell. Time has no meaning during a battle.

The first person to speak was Danny Muggs.

'I got you, Ives.'

No response.

'You're bleedin', bwaay.'

Still nothing from Ives.

'I tell you, your chicken is well and truly cooked,' Danny sneered.

For all the bravado there was in his voice a strong vein of uncertainty.

If Ives was wounded, as it seemed, I had to get round to where he was.

Danny spoke again. 'I got you pegged, Ives. Better give up.'

Ives did not reply. Either he was wounded and could not speak, or he did not wish to reveal his position to this deadly enemy.

I moved slowly round. I had guessed where Danny was, and avoided moving in that direction.

But Danny Muggs was silent now, and that meant only one thing – he too was moving to different positions.

Then I saw Ives, sprawled on the floor, his leg bleeding. His Glock 18 had fallen from his grasp as bullets ripped into his legs.

At the same time, Danny Muggs stepped forward. He could not see me. On his face there was a wide grin of triumph.

'You wasted four of my guys,' Danny said. 'You gotta pay for that.'

He had clearly watched too many late-night Westerns or gangster flicks.

Danny Muggs raised his pistol and pointed it. Ives did not speak, did not plead or ask for mercy.

There was a volley of shots. Ives's body moved in expectation. But it was Danny Muggs whose face showed surprise. He tried to turn, failed to see me with the smoking gun in my hand, and was dead as he hit the floor.

Ives nodded in my direction.

He took out his cell phone.

'You'd better get me out of here, Mr Rubin,' he said.

'No, I think it would be best to put a tourniquet round your leg. You're losing a lot of blood.'

'That can wait,' he said, trying to stand unaided.

'What's the rush, Ives?'

He held up his cell phone. 'Great things, these. I've just given instructions. In five minutes, this place is going to be blown sky high.'

'Dynamite?'

Ives nodded.

I helped him to stand.

'Let's get the fuck out of here,' I said, urgently.

We had almost reached the motor when there was an almighty roar behind us. We turned. The warehouse and all its lethal contents was being destroyed.

As we drove away, me at the wheel, we could hear the distant sound, coming nearer, of police klaxon horns.